BILLIONAIRE BACHELOR:

DIAMOND BRIDAL AGENCY

BOOK 4

EVE BLACK

Billionaire Bachelor: Vitali

Cover design by Sweet n' Spicy Designs.

To all the chocolatiers who make me weak in the knees. You, alone, have fueled me through the writing of this book.

1

Dear Mr. Pavlovich,

I am pleased to inform you that we have selected a bride who matches perfectly the extremely detailed list of requirements you sent. As per your letter, your bride is an attorney, works in Chicago, is of Latin-American heritage, comes from an impoverished family, and is exactly 27 years old.

Though she was hesitant to agree to your desire for anonymity, after taking a total of eight days to review the contract, she has signed it. Because we at Diamond Bridal Agency take our business and your privacy seriously, we ask that you destroy this letter once you have read it.

Your bride, Miss Mariana Sanchez, will arrive in Moscow via private jet at Vnukovo Airport on Saturday of this week, 5:00PM GMT. Please, be advised that any marriage performed in Russia must be followed up, within the month, by an American ceremony—as per Miss Sanchez's personal requirements.

Congratulations and best wishes,
Ms. Alveda Creed, Diamond Bridal Agency

Vitali stared down at the letter in his hand and felt the slow burn of victory scorch his blood.

Finally...she would be his.

Tossing the letter into the fireplace, to destroy it as the extremely strict woman commanded, he turned and made his way to his desk—a large, ornate, black oak antique that he'd won at auction ten years before. It was one of his most prized possessions, something he'd coveted since seeing it in the home of his greatest business rival. And now, it was his.

Just as Mariana Sanchez was his.

Sliding his hand over the top of the desk, he moved toward the windows set into the south side of his immense mansion—one of five. Looking out over the sprawling grounds of his Russian estate, pride filled his chest and a smile cracked his lips.

It was Thursday afternoon, which meant he had less time than he thought before coming face to face with the woman he'd been fantasizing about for two years. But that didn't matter. Once Mariana was in his home, beneath his protection...*beneath him*...he could take all the time in the world. And he would. He'd already waited two years for her, watching her, hungering for her, but keeping his distance. At first, he'd thought his desire for her was a fluke—she wasn't his usual type: tall, shapely but toned, and usually fair-skinned. And, he had been without a woman for a month at that point. But, when he'd started dreaming about her, waking up hard and desperate, he knew she was more than just an object of momentary lust. She'd burrowed deep into his blood, become such a necessary part of him, a part it was becoming ever more difficult to live without. And he didn't want to.

He dreamt about her, woke up aching for her, spent all day wondering about her, and then, once night returned, he'd both dread and anticipate going back to sleep. Because that's where he could have her, where he could lay her down on their bed and make slow, agonizingly sensual love to her.

But it wasn't just her body he craved. When he'd ordered Oleg to do a search on her, he'd known there was no coming back from that, and he was right. Because once he'd learned about the true Mariana Sanchez, the woman beneath the curve hugging suits, the snapping brown eyes and razor-sharp intelligence, he was hooked. Not only had she struggled and fought her way up from a poor neighborhood in Miami to a penthouse in Chicago, she'd grown her law practice from two clients with barely $200,000 between them, to a handful of clients worth $2 billion. She was hardworking, charitable—she gave 30% of her yearly income to women's causes and cancer research—and brilliant. When he'd first seen her, standing before the judge's bench, staring down the defense, he knew there was something in her he had to have for himself. He had to know her. She had an intelligence and confidence he didn't often see in such a scrumptious package.

There would be no other woman for him.

And there would be *no other man for her*.

Too bad he couldn't have claimed her sooner...before she'd sought to move out of his reach. Anger slowly rose to brush against his elation. At first, he'd been able to keep his distance from her, watch over her, tell himself that once he was done with his business in Moscow, he'd head back to the US and finally claim her. Perhaps slowly seduce her with flowers and sumptuous dinners, and then seduce her with touches and kisses—nice and slow, as a woman of her beauty and passion deserved. But...a month of business turned into a shit storm of legal and financial complications —fuck his brother, Dmitri, for screwing up and making things so goddamn difficult. Thank God for Oleg Teleten, black hat "internet spelunker" extraordinaire. With Oleg's skill, Vitali had been able to "keep tabs" on Mariana. Certainly, it was less than legal, but he didn't care. She was his, and it was his duty to make sure she was safe...and that no man ever touched her. If Vitali hadn't been stuck in Moscow cleaning up his brother's mess, he could have already tasted the delights of his woman. Instead, she'd applied to a fucking bridal agency—like it was a fucking job —to find herself a husband.

Burning from within, Vitali began pacing his large office, from windows to windows.

Mariana had offered herself up to some stranger, willingly signing up to be some other man's woman, to allow some other man to have all that Vitali had been waiting so patiently for.

Sucking in a deep breath, he closed his eyes, and images of Mariana flashed through his mind. Long, thick black hair, curvy hips, plump ass, tits big enough to satiate even the most voracious appetite, lips made of pillows and fantasies, and a fiery passion he could see even in the courtroom—where he'd first spied her, tearing apart his company's claim to farmland in Nebraska. He'd hated that she'd won that case—it had cost him $300 million dollars, but he didn't care about that, not after watching her.

And now, all that curvy, sexy, fiery passion was his.

His cock thickened, growing to press against his trousers. He groaned, palming the monster to help alleviate some of the ache, but it did little good. Nothing had, not since that day in court.

A knock at his office door made him call, "Come."

The door opened and Lyuba entered. Lyuba Malikov was his lead attorney, his best legal counsel, and his one-time lover. Tall, red-haired, pouty lips, and chilling blue eyes, Lyuba could have made a career out of killing it in magazine spreads instead of the courtroom. She was lethal, bold, cold, calculating...the perfect attorney. And one of his greatest relationship mistakes. Where she was icy in the courtroom, she was flames in the bedroom, and he'd enjoyed the dichotomy more than once over the five years she'd been in his employ. But no more. After their last encounter in Paris in 2015, where they'd fucked for two days, she'd become more...*complicated.*

During a meeting with Parisian investors, she'd pulled him aside and asked, "When can I tell people about us?"

About *us*? That had been the last thing he'd wanted to hear from her mouth. He wasn't the marrying type, at least not then. And he couldn't imagine himself building a life with Lyuba. She didn't have that...spark, that one thing that lit all of him on fire, not just his cock. That night, he'd ended their love affair, letting her know that she was to remain his lawyer, but any further extracurricular activities were off the table.

Lyuba had looked hurt and fit to murder, but she'd hadn't said a word about it since.

"What is it, Lyuba?" he asked, still vibrating with unspent frustration.

She came to a stop before his desk and crossed her arms, eying him contemplatively.

"You are making a trip into Moscow?" she asked, her blue eyes analyzing him. Then, her gaze dropped to his cock, which was still prominent and throbbing. A flicker of excitement appeared on her face before it was quickly hidden behind her cool façade once again.

He ignored her reaction to him. "Yes, I have business there." He turned away from her and went to sit at his desk, hiding both his now dwindling erection and his agitation with her. What did it matter to her if he were going to Moscow?

She arched an eyebrow. "Business?" she repeated, a question on her pale face.

He nodded then reached for the last stack of paperwork he needed to finish before leaving that evening.

She uncrossed her arms, leaning against his desk, and giving him more than a glimpse down the front of her blouse. "I can clear my schedule, then—"

"No need," he said, interrupting her obvious attempt to reignite the affair that had died a fiery death. "This is *personal* business." He refused to explain further. Again, this was none of her concern. The last thing he wanted to do before meeting Mariana face to face was to deal with Lyuba. Besides that, he didn't want any interruptions. Once Mariana stepped off that plane, he'd whisk her to the priest and put a ring on it, finally claiming what has been his for two years. He wouldn't waste another minute.

He had much planned for his bride...

2

Mariana Sanchez sighed and hit the green button on her cell phone screen, answering the call from her executive assistant...and best friend.

"Mia, is something wrong?" she asked, somewhat relieved to have something to think about besides her impending meeting with the complete stranger she'd agreed to marry.

"No, nothing's wrong, Mari. I just wanted to check in and see how the travelling is going."

Swallowing down the bile, Mariana replied, "I'm still on the plane." It wasn't a lie, she really was still on the plane...but the plane wasn't flying to where Mia thought it was.

"Ooo...I cannot wait to see the pictures of the blue water and sea turtles," her friend practically squealed, and Mariana practically broke and told her the truth. *I'm not going to St. Lucia! I'm going to Russia! To marry a complete and utter stranger! And I don't even know his name!*

But she couldn't say a word about it. She was legally obligated—because she signed a contract—to keep her mouth shut about all matters pertaining to her use of the Diamond Bridal Agency, her match and upcoming marriage to a secretive billionaire, and her trip to Moscow.

"You know I don't plan to do much picture taking, that isn't my thing. I just want to relax," Mariana said, trying to keep her voice even. She hated lying to Mia; Mia had been with her since she was a poor public defender in Miami. They'd climbed to the top together. Mariana would be nothing without Mia. Which made lying to Mia like slicing away at her own flesh and blood.

"Girl, you know I don't care about you taking pictures. You've earned this sabbatical! A month on an island, laying in the sand, drinking fruity *cock*tails, and chasing some cock..."

Mariana snorted, rolling her eyes. "Sounds like you're the one in need of a sabbatical."

Mia laughed, her throaty chuckle filling Mariana with a sense of peace she desperately needed.

"I promise to drink lots of cocktails—"

"And chase some cock," Mia interjected.

Mariana laughed, and the tight band around her chest loosened a little. "There will be no cock chasing, Mia. That's not me, you know that." As a matter of fact, Mariana had been so busy climbing the corporate ladder, she'd had no time to climb anything else, including a man.

That was part of the reason she'd contacted the Diamond Bridal Agency in the first place. She'd woken up one morning, walked through her large, beautifully furnished penthouse apartment and realized how empty it all was. What was the point of having so much wealth and success without someone to share it with?

After doing some discreet digging, she'd found the exclusive and incredibly picky bridal agency. Using a meeting with a client for an excuse, she flew to Houston where she met with a pinch-faced woman named Alveda Creed. Alveda conducted an extensive and, at times, embarrassing interview, and finally informed her that she'd advanced to the next portion of the application process: the thorough physical. The doctor performed a highly-detailed examination, tested her for all sorts of diseases, and finally announced her healthy and STD free. Also...he'd made sure Ms. Creed knew that Mariana was a virgin.

What the hell did that have to do with anything? Did that really matter? Apparently so, because Ms. Creed made sure to include that information in Mariana's dossier. After that, Mariana had flown home, a little put out by the whole experience, and not really expecting much. Not more than a week later, she'd received a letter—by snail-mail—from the agency, saying she'd been matched and that she would receive the contract, via courier, within the week.

And now, she was two hours away from touching down in Moscow to meet and then marry a man she could only guess about. Mrs. Creed—the dragon lady who ran the agency—shared the barest of details about her potential groom. He was filthy rich, from Russia, had a particular list of requirements for his potential bride—and *she* matched every single one of them.

Fate? Chance? Luck?

She didn't know whether she was fated to apply to the agency at the right time or whether she'd been lucky to find a man who wanted someone just like her. Either way, she'd signed on the dotted line, and there was no going back.

"Shit," Mia said from the other line, snapping Mariana back into their conversation. "Bonnie just got here. I need to get going." Bonnie, or Bonita, was Mia's daughter, the light of her life, and the terror of the cul-de-sac where she and her mother lived. At four years old, the little girl was all sass and smarts, just like her mother.

"Okay. Give *mi sobrina* a kiss from *Tia* Mari," Mariana said, holding back a wash of tears and the urge to blurt everything to her friend who was getting farther away by the second.

"You know I will," Mia replied.

They ended the call and Mariana laid her head back against the soft leather seat. Taking a deep, calming breath, she let her gaze slowly take in the luxury and decadence of the private jet. As a multi-millionaire owner of a multi-national corporate law firm, she was used to flying to and from trials and consultations in her clients' private jets, but nothing compared to this...

Crème and mocha trimmed every surface. Lush high pile carpets absorbed the sound of the engines and cradled her feet. Mahogany cupboards and tables added just the right amount of masculinity to the space. She felt like she was in someone's private bedroom, not in a tin can flying 30,000 feet over the face of the planet.

When she'd arrived at the airport the night before, she'd been greeted by a man wearing a black suit, sunglasses, and a severe expression—like he'd wiped his ass with hot sauce. That man introduced himself as Gregor, escorted her to the plane and, while she picked her jaw up off the carpet, he'd disappeared into the cockpit without a single word in her direction. So, she couldn't even ask the man about his employer. Her future husband. The flight attendant wouldn't look her in the eye. She would serve Mariana whatever she requested, but if she tried to ask the woman—whose silver nametag read "Petya"—about her boss, she would smile, then politely excuse herself.

What had the man done? Demand absolute anonymity, even from his employees?

She shrugged. At least they were loyal.

Another two hours passed in a slog of uncertainty, anxiety, fear, excitement, and finally resignation. This was what she wanted, what she'd expected when she'd taken the leap into the arranged marriage pool. And when the plane landed and taxied to an airstrip off the main, busy runway, she told herself she wasn't shaking because she was nervous...

The plane slowed to a halt. When the bumps and whirring of throttling down the engine were finished, the man—Gregor—reappeared. Flashing an expression of cool antipathy, he gave her a single nod, as if saying "well done, you've completed the first challenge."

What an ass. No, that wasn't fair to cold, square-faced Gregor. The man didn't care who she was or why she was there, he was just doing his job. Just like the flight attendant.

Hoping her legs would hold her, Mariana stood and straightened the hip hugging pencil skirt she'd finally settled on after three hours of trying on outfits and discarding them. It wasn't business attire—it showed way too much ass cheek—but it was the best attempt at pleasing the man she was going to spend the rest of her life with. First impressions, and all that. Hopefully, he liked plush women as much as he liked plush carpets.

Gregor opened the door and stopped her before she could make a break for it.

"Mr. Pavlovich is waiting for you at the hotel," Gregor intoned, his strong Russian accent only emphasizing his chilly demeanor. If Spanish was a language of love and passion, Russian was a language of ice and rocks.

Mr. Pavlovich? So that was the name of her husband-to-be. It was a good, strong name, at least. Mariana Pavlovich... *Wait! Where have I heard that last name before?*

"Come," Gregor said, snatching the answer from the tip of her brain. "We should not keep him waiting. He is most eager to see you."

Somewhat relieved that she wouldn't have to meet her groom just then, she let herself relax a bit. Until she realized what else he'd said: *He is most eager to see you...*

A fist of anxiety and self-doubt punched her in the gut. He was eager *now*, but would he feel the same way once he actually met her? No, she wasn't ugly—had been called pretty on more than one occasion—but she wasn't billionaire marriage material. Not really. Not when he could have picked any number of Russian beauties to marry. Sure, she had no idea what he looked like, he could probably be a Hugh Hefner-esque man, old and creepy, but his money could have bought him more than enough marriage-minded women.

So why did he go through the agency? Why did he ask for a woman of Latin-American heritage?

Gregor cleared his throat, and Mariana remembered he had spoken.

"That's fine," she replied, offering the man a polite smile. "I assume transportation has been provided." She was using her corporate lawyer tone, and she didn't regret it. It was her go-to when she felt out of her element—like when she was in a new country, surrounded by hostiles, and headed into the den of the bear!

"Of course, Miss Sanchez," Gregor said, indicating that she should follow behind him as he descended the steel stairs someone had rolled up against the plane. Thankfully, her mental image of Russia wasn't what greeted her. She always thought of the country as cold, frigid. But the early evening sun shone down on them, and the air was crisp yet refreshing, like the first bite of autumn before the lion of winter. Mariana pulled her light coat tighter around her shoulders and tried to hold her hair out of her eyes, but the wind whipping across the tarmac ruined any chance of her making her hair behave. Thick, straight as a pin, and long, her only hope of saving herself from embarrassment was to wind it into a braid. But what kind of picture would that present to her future husband? The Latina with the wild black hair, black V-neck cashmere sweater, and blood-colored skirt; the very picture of spicy.

Gregor escorted her to a waiting black car and she climbed into the backseat. It was as comfortable as her seat on the plane. Once her luggage was loaded into the trunk, Gregor climbed into the passenger seat, nodding to the driver who was just as Friday-faced as Gregor. They left the airport and proceeded into Moscow.

Never having set foot in Russia before, everything was new to her; big buildings, a purple and red sunset, and glittering but intermittent street lights.

So, this will be my home for the next month...

She realized the discordance of it; she was burning with excitement—with a scooch of trepidation—about this new adventure, but she was also chilled by the anticipation and fear of the unknown. As she stared out the window at the busy city buzzing by, her heart climbing higher into her throat, Mariana couldn't help but wonder: *Have I made a mistake?*

3

Mariana tried to hide her shock at the size of the hotel they were pulling up to, but she failed.

"Holy shit," she murmured, and Gregor ignored her.

The driver stopped the car and Gregor got out, coming to the back to open the door for her.

Swallowing the ball of uncertainty in her throat, she forced herself to slide from the seat and put her feet on the ground. Her three-inch, black Louboutins had been a laborious choice as well—though they weren't practical travel wear, they were certainly eye-catching. Again, she was hoping that whoever her fiancé was, he appreciated all the effort she went to in order to be appealing.

Standing, Mariana's gaze landed on the doors leading into the hotel lobby. Two men stood, dressed in black coats and black ties, staring at her with bored expressions. If this is what men in Russia were like, she didn't hold out much hope for a warm welcome from her fiancé. The men at the door wore name tags, so they weren't like Gregor—whatever

Gregor was—and they were holding the doors open for her. With a flick of his wrist, Gregor indicated she should go ahead of him, and she did, throwing back her shoulders, forcing a rod of steel and determination down her back, and pushing her chin into the air. What the hell was she doing acting like a frightened little girl? She was a powerful, professional woman!

You're damn right!

With a little more brass than she'd felt since leaving Chicago, Mariana strode through the hotel doors and into the lobby, which looked more like a museum housing Russian historical artifacts than a hotel lobby. Gold and glass were everywhere, and the furnishings were dark wood covered in blacks and deep reds. It was beautiful, flashy, just the kind of place a billionaire would stay when he was in town.

Gregor led her to the golden elevator, and Mariana stepped into it without hesitation. But she held her breath all the way up to the top floor. The penthouse suite. Of course, a billionaire would want the biggest, most elegant of rooms.

What better place to meet a complete stranger?

And consummate a marriage? Struck by that thought, Mariana, again, wondered about her groom. Was he handsome? Ugly? Old? Young? An asshole? Charming? Would she like him on sight or would it take months or even years? And what would he think about her? Did he have all the same questions about her?

The questions swirled about in her head, making her dizzy—not that holding her breath helped. She exhaled, then took a deep, steadying inhale.

This was the first step into a new life, a life of something with more meaning than steel and concrete offices and depositions.

As the elevator dinged, indicating their floor, Mariana straightened her shoulders and stared straight ahead, both eager and terrified of her first sight of Mr. Pavlovich.

But the foyer was empty. The elevator doors opened into an empty vestibule of sorts. Beside her, Gregor cleared his throat.

"Please, Miss Sanchez," he said, stretching his arm out before them. "I will send up your bags."

Wait...he wasn't staying? He was just leaving her there? Alone?

He must have read the burgeoning panic on her face because he intoned, "Mr. Pavlovich wishes to meet you. Alone." His expression one of stone, Mariana knew she was on her own, which was ridiculous—why did she feel as though Gregor's presence would make her first meeting with her future husband any easier?

Stop being a wuss! Suck it up! You've faced down entire teams of corporate legal counsel, snapping their jaws at you to intimidate you into settling out of court. You can handle one *man.*

Somewhat emboldened by her internal pep talk, she offered Gregor a single nod then stepped off the elevator and onto the white marble floors of the penthouse.

As the elevator doors slid shut behind her, she steeled herself and walked forward, her heels *click-clacking* on the marble. Beyond the vestibule the room opened into a space large enough to hold court. Furnished in creams, golds, burnished reds and yellows, the room reminded her of a sunset. Without thought, she tugged off her coat, tossed it over a chair to her right, and her feet carried her further into the suite, her mind still swirling. For all her questions, they would be answered soon—as soon as she saw the man she was to marry.

Mariana stopped in the middle of the large, unoccupied room, and she held her breath. Where was Mr. Pavlovich? She'd expected him to greet her at the airport, but he hadn't. Then, she expected him to meet her in the lobby, but he hadn't. Then—though she probably should have guessed—she'd expected him to meet her off the elevator. He hadn't. Already, her intended was proving unpredictable.

She didn't like that; feeling unsteady, as though she were treading over sand instead of marble.

Deep rumbling emanated from a room to the right. She turned, spying a closed door. Suddenly her every sense was tuned to the slab of dark wood separating her from whom she suspected was Mr. Pavlovich. Without a doubt her future husband was in there, probably conducting business —billionaires had to work sometime, right? Not wanting to interrupt whatever was going on, Mariana stood still, listening.

The man was speaking in Russian, his voice deep enough to raise goosebumps over her skin, and she trembled. It was the first sound to ever do that. And if his voice could do that...

More deep rumbling, louder this time. Whatever was going on, he didn't sound pleased.

Oh, great. He's gonna be all pissed when he meets me. My luck he'll take one look at me and chuck me out on my fat ass. Attorney Mariana Sanchez was all badass confidence in gray suits, standing before a courtroom, tearing contracts to shreds, but here, now...she was simply lonely Mariana Sanchez, desperate single woman, hoping to make a connection that would last a lifetime. She'd never been so scared—or so thrilled—in all her life.

Suddenly in need of fresh air, Mariana turned to find a door to the terrace—every penthouse had a terrace. Finding it, she *click-clacked* her way to it, throwing open the door. The chill of the night air slapped her face, and she sucked in a shocked breath. It was bracing. Mind-clearing.

But that clarity turned to mush in an instant. He was there... behind her. He hadn't made a sound, hadn't announced his presence, she simply *felt* him, watching her. Why wasn't he saying something? Was something wrong? Was he taking her measure before she could even gaze upon his face? Again, her thoughts raced with questions only one man could answer.

This is it! Time to put up or shut the hell up!

Holding her breath, Mariana squared her shoulders and pushed away from the railing where she'd been leaning. Turning, she nearly lost all ability to think—before her was the most beautiful man she'd ever seen.

Hair so black it was nearly pitch, and eyes that burned the color of priceless emeralds. Tall, with broad shoulders that strained the confines of his obviously tailored suit coat. She would bet a month's worth of retainer fees that beneath the crisp white shirt he wore, every inch of him was hardened steel, covered in toned flesh. Chiseled jaw, straight nose, and full, smirking lips. The man was a god among men, a man who made her heart thud wildly and her belly clench heatedly.

And he was staring at her with a chilling intensity in his eyes.

"Hello, Mariana," he drawled, the corners of his sensual mouth rising to flash his perfect white teeth—like a wolf brandishing his most menacing weapons.

She blinked at him, her voice lost somewhere beneath her utter shock at how gorgeous he was, and how her body was responding to him—as if it were caught up in the snare of his masculinity.

His mesmerizing gaze swept over her, taking in the flare of her hips, the swell of her breasts, and finally landing on her face once more. "I have been waiting for you..."

4

Mine, his mind growled even as he smiled at his woman across the terrace. He'd known she arrived, had been waiting for her, but a call from Lyuba had curtailed his first official meeting with the woman he'd been hungering to taste for two years.

But now, she was here, staring at him, her big chocolate eyes wide, her lush, pink lips parted in surprise, and her long black hair waving like ink ribbons in the chill night wind. The light from the LED sconces on either side of the door did little to illuminate her, but he didn't need any light to know each feature, each curve, each hollow of her face and body. He'd memorized her. Studied her.

As he'd done with everything he'd ruthlessly pursued.

She was wearing a tight, form-fitting skirt that hid nothing from his gaze. The heels on her feet emphasized the shapeliness of her calves, and the length of her legs. The light sweater she wore covered most of her breasts, but he could see the swell of them beneath the soft looking fabric.

Perfectly sized for his large hands. What color were her nipples? Would they be a dark pink, or more a chocolate brown to accent the creamy brown of her skin? Mariana was a vision, his every fantasy come to life, and he couldn't wait to pull her into him, feel her warmth against him. God, it was a yearning he was having a difficult time ignoring.

Willing his heart to beat a steady rhythm and his cock to settle the hell down, he offered Mariana a slow, appreciative smile. "Hello, Mariana," he drawled, his mouth forming words even as his hands ached to reach out and touch in her a *proper* greeting. Fuck proper. He wanted to bend her over the railing and pound into her hot wetness until she screamed—and all of Moscow knew she was his. "I have been waiting for you..." *For too fucking long.*

She blinked, snapping her mouth shut as if to keep from blurting something.

"How was your trip?" he asked, his voice a little deeper than he'd anticipated, but what could be expected? He was holding back two years' worth of sexual tension. "I hope you aren't too tired after your journey to join me for dinner." *One step at a time, Vitali. Feed her...before you feast on her.*

Mariana's gaze landed on his mouth, laser-focused on his lips as he spoke.

As if snapped from a fog, she lifted her chin and pinned him with a cool expression. "I believe I am at a disadvantage; you know my name, but I don't know yours," she intoned, her husky voice only succeeding in stirring up the blood in his cock again. What would that husky voice of hers do when she was moaning beneath him as he thrust into her? His belly tightened, the ache in his balls growing all the more excruciating.

"Vitali," he answered, watching as she tucked an errant lock of dark hair behind her ear. So fucking sexy. "Vitali Pavlovich."

"Vitali," she said, almost hesitantly. The sound of his name on her lips—in that fucking husky voice—flipped a switch in his brain. Fuck waiting until tomorrow to marry this woman, he'd have the priest meet them here, in the penthouse. They'd be married within the hour...then, he could take his sweet time, getting to know every hot, silky, curvy inch of his new wife.

Pulling his phone from his breast pocket, he dialed Gregor. In Russian, he commanded, "Call Father Itszack. Have him meet us here now. Offer him another ten-thousand in church donations for his expediency." As he spoke, he watched Mariana watching him, her soft brown eyes taking in his face, continuing to watch his mouth—she seemed particularly taken with his lips.

The feeling is mutual. Her lips were the perfect shape, a lush bow he wanted to plunder.

After hanging up with Gregor, he offered his bride another smile, one he hoped wasn't loaded with the sexual ferocity he was feeling in his blood. It wouldn't do to scare her off before he had the chance to seduce her as he'd been wanting to do for far too long.

"Come inside," he coaxed. "We'll have dinner brought up, and we can chat."

She raised a single inky eyebrow, her shoulders relaxing a mite. "Alright."

Reaching out, Vitali waited for her to take his hand. She gave it a quick glance before bringing her own hand up to place in his. Electricity on par with a lightning strike snapped through him, making his breath catch. Her eyes widened at the contact, her mouth opening on a silent gasp.

She felt it, too, that connection, that instant attraction.

He fought the urge to growl, instead, he waited for her to say something—anything—to help him dispel the thrumming in his ears, the sound of his heart pounding in his chest.

Damn...this woman...

As if taking his direction, Mariana led the way off the terrace and into the penthouse. He'd picked the largest penthouse in the city, not because he needed the space, but because he deserved the luxury. He could afford to buy the whole hotel if he wanted—he'd worked hard for every single billion of his billion-dollar empire, and now he would spend a little time enjoying the fruits of his labors...with this woman beside him.

Once inside the penthouse, he took over, leading her to the large leather couches in the center of the large room. The couches were set in a semi-circle, facing the windows over the terrace, and there was a long, low coffee table in front of them. He waited for her to take a seat—watching her ass as she did so—and then, took the seat beside her. Close enough to smell her scent; something warm, inviting... wholly intoxicating. Vitali let his gaze roam over her as she sat, stiffly, taking in the room, obviously avoiding looking at him.

Was she nervous? She had no reason to be, and he wanted her to be comfortable—*needed* her to be comfortable. The urge to see to his woman's comfort—to her *every need*—was overwhelming. And he dare not look closely at why.

Leaning back and crossing his leg, ankle over knee, he forced himself to relax. He could tell his own tension was only feeding hers; her body fairly vibrated with anxiety, and her eyes flicked from surface to surface, trying to find something to help ease that anxiety.

Ease her in, Vitali...

"I want you to be comfortable around me," he said, his voice immediately making her stiffen further. No, this wasn't how it was supposed to be. "Please, Mariana," he leaned forward and waited for her to turn to him. She took a deep breath and finally turned her head to meet his gaze.

Beautiful.

"Vitali," she clipped, her nervousness showing in her voice.

"I think that I need to explain some things; about who I am and why you are here."

Again, she cocked that sexy eyebrow. "I am here because I fit your requirements to a T."

There was that spice he'd been missing since she arrived. He chuckled. "*Da*, and there is a reason for that..."

She turned her body toward him, her curiosity getting the better of her wariness. "Oh?"

He nodded, quirking his lips into a lopsided smile. "I wanted you," he said, simply.

Confusion pulled her eyebrows down into a furrow, and he almost gave into another chuckle.

"The Diamond Bridal Agency is known for its secretiveness, exclusivity, and rigorous screening of applicants. One thing they absolutely assured me was that it was all anonymous, even going so far as to keep your name a secret," she remarked, her voice slowly building in volume. "So, how is it that you knew me and that you would want me?" She said that last two words with acidic disbelief.

So, his beautiful handful didn't believe that he would want her. Well, he'd just have to prove how wrong she was.

Sliding toward her along the leather seat, he didn't stop until his thigh touched hers, the heat of her body scalding him, burning through him like a fire through a parched forest. He could hear her drag in a breath and hold it, and she tipped her head back to look up into his face. Her eyes, once again, landed on his mouth. He smiled wolfishly.

"I've wanted you from the moment I saw you," he murmured, his voice low, "and now that I have you, I can't wait another moment to kiss you."

Without giving her the time to pull away, Vitali reached up to cradle her face in his hands. She breathed out, her chest rising and falling in sharp inhalations, and a deep pink flush rose over her cheeks. God, but she was lovely.

"Y-you want to kiss me?" she asked, her eyes wide, uncertainty flashing through the mocha depths.

He lowered his head, stopping just short of brushing his lips against hers. Her eyelids grew heavy, and his breathing followed suit.

"I want to do so much more than that, *tol'ko moya*." My only. The thick lashes that fanned her cheeks fluttered, and a dark glinting filled her eyes. He drew her closer, could feel the heat of her breath on his skin as she shuddered against him, the generous globes of her breasts pressing against the hardness of his chest. *Exquisite.* Her beautiful, soft pink lips parted, as if in invitation, and the world seemed to quiet in awe of what he was about to taste—

The penthouse landline rang, the shrill sound startling in the heavy silence of the room.

"Shit," he muttered in Russian, pulling away reluctantly. The tension still coiled in his gut—and lower—he stood to answer the phone, ready to damn whoever was on the other end of the line. Before he turned away from Mariana, he could see a sort of mask slip down over her expressive face, effectively hiding the fiery woman he'd nearly kissed behind a mien of professionalism and indifference. Like a lawyer preparing to face the judge.

He hid a grin, one he knew would appear predatory, ravenous. He would enjoy peeling away the lawyer to get to the fire beneath.

5

Saved by the bell, she thought, dragging in desperate gulps of air to fill her burning lungs. She couldn't help but watch him—Vitali—as he strode across the room to answer the phone, the bottom of his suit coat hid his ass from her view, but she'd be fooling herself if she thought there wasn't a honed, rock hard booty behind those tailored slacks.

She couldn't tear her eyes from him. The black of his hair glinted beneath the light of the giant chandelier overhead, the thick lustrous locks begging for her fingers to slide through them. They'd be soft, silky, the perfect handhold for when she lay under him, a slave to his demands on her body. He'd brush his sexy lips over her neck, murmuring dirty words to her in Russian, then he'd press her down, putting all his weight on her, and she'd mewl, moaning like a cat in heat, and then he'd drag his mouth down, taking her nipple—

Whoa! Where had that come from? She'd never let a man put his arm around her waist before, and now she was having dirty, breathtakingly vivid thoughts about a man she'd only known for twenty minutes? But, hell, what a man he was. Her gaze remained on his back, admiring the height, the breadth, the very strength pulsing from his frame. His broad shoulders filled that coat nicely—perfectly—and the way he smelled... God damn, she was in trouble. How had she ended up here, with him? He was what erotic romance novels were made of, the stuff of naughty dreams and dirty imaginings. And yet, he was just across the room, speaking into the receiver in that deep, rumbling, sexy as hell voice of his. Her body in flames, the very core of her roiling—in the anticipation of pleasure and the twinge of fear, she held her breath as he terminated the call and turned back toward her, his eyes pinning her to the luxurious leather couch like a stick pin through a mounted butterfly. How could a single look from Vitali have reduced her to a babbling, fumbling, practically whimpering lamb—in the sights of a ruthless predator, no less?

Get it together, Mari! Yeah, but how was *that* supposed to work? The sexiest man she'd ever laid eyes on was now stalking across the room toward her, a sly smile on his gorgeous lips... The same lips that had told her he'd *wanted* her since he'd seen her...and that he *wanted* to kiss her. *Her!* Mariana Sanchez, chubby Latina, the bookworm, the nerd, the hopeless spinster, without a single notch in her bedpost.

Suddenly, a band of iron fused itself to her back, strengthening her flagging resolve. She was here, with him, because she'd decided that enough was enough—she was tired of being lonely, of her life being one rut after another. And, from the looks of him, Vitali Pavlovich was the perfect man to pull her from her ruts and help her to realize the life she'd been skirting until now.

He was the sexiest damn man in the whole world. Wasn't that a bonus? And they were getting married—but first...

"Before we go any further," she said, her all-business tone making its appearance—thank God!— "I think we need to discuss the details of the contract." That got her another raised eyebrow, this one nearly flying into his hairline.

A simmering, intense look flashed through his eyes before being doused by that same chilly intensity she'd seen when she spied him for the first time. Good. She needed him to back away, give her some breathing room. She couldn't think if she overheated.

"A lawyer through and through..." he drawled, raking his emerald gaze over her before sitting down in the upholstered chair across from the couch. He leaned back in the seat, crossed his leg over his knee, and placed the flat of his hands on the upholstered arms of the chair. Once again Mariana couldn't tear her gaze away; the man was all power and sexual potency, even when he was giving the impression of ease. Simply sitting there, Vitali gave off wave after wave of dangerous, intoxicating, and utterly palpable masculinity. Strangely disappointed that he hadn't sat next to her again, and angry at her disappointment, she charged ahead.

Biting the inside of her cheek to steady herself, she met his gaze head-on. "Not just a lawyer, the best damn lawyer, under 30, in Chicago." *That* was her fiery, defiant voice, one she'd usually kept at bay, but around Vitali, she was losing her cool. *Dammit, Mari!* Clearing her throat, and checking her attitude, she continued, "I took my time looking over the contract provided by Ms. Creed."

Vitali didn't bat an eye, didn't move a muscle, didn't even seem to be breathing. It was unnerving, how he could stare at her so intently. Swallowing, she waited another moment to give him a chance to chime in. When he didn't, she cocked an eyebrow then tipped her head, ever so slightly, in the way that usually unsettled her opposition.

"This is the part where you ask me if I have any questions," she drawled, crossing her arms over her chest in a show of nonchalance she wasn't feeling.

Nothing. The man continued to watch her, his eyes never leaving her face, and she couldn't figure out what the hell he was thinking about. Moments ago, the man was fire, but now...he was ice. Perhaps talk of business wasn't the way to go.

But she persisted, because, while she was shit at relationships, she was a goddess in the courtroom. "While I agreed to marry you—and all the conditions that come with that change in status, I think it best that we take some time to get to know one another before we consummate—"

Vitali shot forward in his seat, his eyes blazing. "No," he barked. And she felt the edge of her restraint slip.

"What do you mean, no?" she asked, her voice lowering in warning, like a lioness voicing her displeasure.

He rose to his full height, dwarfing her, where she sat on the couch. So, she stood up, too. He was still a head taller than her, though, so she craned her head to meet his gaze, which was pouring cold fire into her.

He stepped around the coffee table with a predatory grace that struck her dumb—something that was happening much too frequently as of late. Once he was standing before her, he reached up and grasped her chin in his large, rough, hot hand, holding her in place. She bit her lip, uncertainty and wariness warring against her desire to remain calm. His green eyes followed the movement of her mouth as she nibbled nervously. Fire bloomed to life in his gaze, and he growled. "I mean that I have already waited two years for you, Mariana. I refuse to wait another day to make you mine."

THE URGE TO TAKE HER BOTTOM LIP BETWEEN HIS OWN TEETH throbbed through him with a crashing wave of desire. She didn't know the power she wielded over him; her movements and reactions were not some elaborate yet subtle form of seduction. She was guileless but undeniably compelling.

He refused to let her wiggle her luscious ass out of consummating their marriage. Even now, every instinct to claim her roared from within him, snapping its jaws, unsheathing its claws, desperate to rip that skirt from her body, spread her thighs apart, and lap at her cunny like a starving beast.

His cock raged just as hard, and he knew he was letting his body rule his brain, but the look of defiance on her face made the beast within him roar all the more. What he wouldn't give to see that expression melt into one of utter surrender.

Squaring his shoulders, he scrubbed a hand down his face, turning away from her to put some distance between them.

From behind him, her husky voice slid over his senses like a silk sheet. “Two years? I’ve only known you for half an hour...” He could feel her gaze boring into him, her puzzlement out of place in her usually confident demeanor—not that she’d let him know he’d shaken her, even a little bit. The sound of her breath catching brought him around to look at her. She’d gone pale, her lustrous eyes wide, and her mouth set in a grim line.

“Now I know why your name sounds so familiar—you’re Vitali Pavlovich, owner of Trans-Global Corporation,” she said, almost accusingly. “I won a case against your company in 2016.” She gasped, her color returning. “Is that what this is about? You wanting to get back at me for winning in court?” Her voice had taken on a disgusted tone that pulled at his already taut nerves.

“*Blyad.* Hell no,” he growled. “I would never take your victory and taint it like that. You won that case, fair.” Something in his voice must’ve been convincing because her shoulders relaxed and her stance eased—just enough for her to cross her arms again. Her breasts heaved upward, nearly toppling over the neckline of her sweater.

Fuck me.

“Fine, then what is this about? I never met *you*, you sent your lackeys—and that female Terminator—to do the negotiating and litigation.”

He fought the urge to smirk at her description of Lyuba. It was a fitting one.

“*Da.* I am usually hands-off during court cases in the U.S.”

She gave a quick nod. "So. Explain..." she commanded, her hands dropping to plant firmly on the curves of her hips. He knew what she meant; how could he possibly want her without actually having met her?

He'd never been one to pull his punches—as Americans would say—and he'd never denied himself anything as achingly long as he'd denied himself Mariana.

"During the litigation phase of the trial, I snuck into the back of the courtroom. I wanted to see the woman who had tied my multi-million-dollar legal team in knots. My first sight of you pulled the rug out from under me; you were wearing a black skirt, white blouse, and blood-red blazer... I nearly climbed out of my skin with the need to know who you were. When Byron Dreven, lead counsel in that case, told me *you* were the opposing counsel, I knew I was well and truly fucked."

He stepped toward her, the need to touch her overwhelming him. He reached out and slid the pad of his finger over her cheek. She shivered.

"You weren't just the most gorgeous woman I'd ever seen, I knew that you were intelligent, clever, driven, and passionate—all things I wanted in the woman who would share my bed."

6

Vitali watched a flurry of emotions tumble through her expression; her chocolate-coffee eyes filling with confusion, then realization, then wariness.

"I see," she said, her voice breathy. So, she wasn't as unaffected as she'd like him to believe. Good. "But how did I end up here? As far as I know, the Diamond Bridal Agency is completely anonymous. Either this was a huge coincidence, or Ms. Creed is running a shoddy business."

Vitali chuckled, running his thumb over her cheek again, just to watch her pupils dilate again.

"I don't believe in coincidences," he replied. "I believe in going after what I want, and I wanted you."

The vixen bit her bottom lip again, and this time, Vitali's thumb traced the indent of her teeth in the plump flesh. A groan lodged in his throat, behind the deep breath he had to take to keep from falling over her in his eagerness to taste her.

Mariana tried pulling away, but Vitali placed a hand on her waist to keep her in place. Her soft gasp made his cock jump.

"That doesn't explain how you knew who I was—out of all the applications, you chose mine. And, how did we end up at the same bridal agency? There has to be more than just the one. You could have picked any one of them." From the weight of her tone, he knew she was calculating the probabilities even as she spoke the questions. God, but she was sharp.

"I picked that one because you did. I knew you'd applied there, and so I contacted the agency, gave them a list of very specific requirements—basically you without the benefit of your name—and waited. Ms. Creed matched us within the week."

Vitali watched the light flick on in her mind; her eyes flew wide in shock then narrowed in fierce anger. His heart leapt, a strange ache pulsing against his ribs.

"You knew? And so, you...what, laid a trap for me?" she practically hissed. She tried pulling away again, but Vitali strengthened his hold on her chin and her waist. He'd be damned if he let her go now.

"It's only a trap if you don't want to get caught. You knew you were signing up to marry a stranger. I wanted you," he said simply. "I couldn't stand the thought of some other man having what I'd been slavering over for nearly two years. So, I did what I had to do to get you here, with me, right where you belong."

Her eyes flashing defiance—brilliant, scorching fire—she parted her lips to, no doubt, tell him where to stick his misogyny, and the beast that had waited two years to taste her finally slipped loose of its cage.

With a growl, he bent down and took her lips, hungrily. Invading the warmth and decadent sweetness with his tongue, he lapped at her, devouring her, begging her to yield to him, to give herself over to the pleasure he could offer her. She stiffened, shock vibrating through her, but then she melted into him, meeting his tongue with her own. Groaning deep in her throat, she placed her hands on his chest and slid them up to wrap around the back of his neck. It was her turn to hold him in place—he wasn't going anywhere anyway. He was finally kissing her, and it was heaven.

Deepening the kiss, his stroked his left hand up her side until his thumb brushed the underside of her breast. She moaned—his woman...she was going up in flames from a single kiss. How would she be, fully naked, in his arms? He would thrust into her, sheathing himself inside her, and she'd come apart, exploding. It would be glorious, like the most erotic masterpiece any man could paint.

His mind and his cock both ravenous for that sight, he dropped his other hand from her face to join the hand at her breasts.

Before he could cup the lush mounds as he so desperately wanted, she stiffened again, this time dropping her hands to his chest to push him. He let her.

Breath heaving, she stared up at him, her eyes dark, lips swollen and kiss ravaged. The vision she made; her face flushed, her eyes and lips begging for his kiss again, was almost too much to bear. But he would...because something was wrong.

Catching his breath, he forced his hands to fall to his sides, where he clenched them to keep from reaching out to her again.

"That... That was amazing," she breathed, her voice huskier than he'd ever heard it. It stirred his blood, making ever more of the precious life force rush to his groin.

Calm down, dammit! You will have her soon. Give her time... He had to remember that she was a gift, something he'd earned for all the hard work and suffering he'd endured. She was the culmination of a life of sacrifice and diligence. Vitali looked down at her—a renewed sense of awe blinding him to all else but her.

"*Da*, it was...amazing." Though amazing couldn't completely describe what he'd felt, it was a good enough start. Mind-blowing. Earth-shattering. Heart-pounding. Devastating. All words to better describe what that kiss had been. "But I can see something is the matter," he drawled, leading her back to the couch where he waited for her to sit before taking the seat beside her.

Mariana clasped her hands in her lap then took a deep breath.

"If you read all the documentation on the agency, you know their stipulations regarding the...err...sexual status of their applicants."

He blinked at her, uncertain of where she was going. "You're a virgin."

A becoming blush colored her cheeks a rich, burnished red, and she bit her lip again, nodding. "Yes, I am."

He cocked his head, his gaze raking over her features. "Is that a problem?" he asked, wondering if her nervousness had finally made its appearance. What a damn fine time for coyness.

She shook her head. "No, not really—at least...not for me..."

Understanding dawned. A smile slowly spread over his face. "You're worried that I will find you...*lacking* in the bedroom."

She squared her shoulders, tipping her chin up in a show of daring. "As I said," she began, her voice sharp, "it isn't a problem for me. I am well aware of my inexperience—not that I am unwilling to learn, on the contrary, I believe that I can be an apt pupil...given the right...*incentives*." Mariana dropped her voice to a low, sultry purr, and he about shook off his restraint to show her just how good a *teacher* he was.

He cleared his throat, offering her what he hoped was a reassuring smile.

"Good."

She raised a sculpted eyebrow, clearly disbelieving his acceptance. "You don't mind my lack of sexual experience?"

He shook his head and leaned forward, placing his large hand over the two in her lap. "Not at all, Mariana. As a matter of fact, it is incredibly arousing to know that you are untouched by any other man, that your flesh is mine to tease..." He reached out, sliding his knuckles up her arm. Goosebumps left a trail in his wake. "And that every sensation you experience, will be something that only I have awakened in you. It's heady...intoxicating. I cannot wait for our *lessons* to begin." He knew he was being intense, that the very air around him was thrumming with the power of his desire and his need for her, but he couldn't stop it. He'd been holding back for two years—too damn long—and she was right there... She wanted him; he could see it in her eyes, could taste it on her lips, and in the thrusts of her tongue. He could seduce her, make her as desperate for him as he was for her. All he had to do was kiss her again...

As if hearing his thoughts, she pulled away, her gorgeous face set in a hard mask.

"Before we begin your *lessons*, I require that we fulfil the terms of the contract first. There will be a wedding ceremony," she said—the lawyer returning with a vengeance.

He smirked, admiring her all the more.

"Agreed," he intoned, just before the suite phone rang—again. Having expected this call, he wasn't angry, more like excited.

Rising from the couch, Vitali strode the phone, answering it.

At the voice on the other line, he smiled into the receiver... It was almost like the *heavens* were smiling on him, too.

7

Holy shit, holy shit, holy shit!

That kiss rocked her world, tilted its axis, and threw her orbit into the heart of the unknown universe. Still in shock, she raised a trembling hand to press her fingers against her lips. They were swollen...from his kiss. A tingle of awareness zapped through her, trailing electric fingers up her spine. Mariana gazed across the room to the man who had literally taken her breath away, and her body responded to the sight of him alone. Unlike last time, when he'd stood with his back to her, this time, he stood, staring at her, his eyes lit with an emerald flame—burning so hot she could feel it where she sat. Moisture gathered between her thighs, not a wholly surprising occurrence, the man had basically fucked her with his mouth.

What will it feel like to truly be fucked by this man?

Just then, his words sank in through the haze of wantonness... *"I couldn't stand the thought of some other man having what I'd been slavering over for nearly two years..."* The man *had* set a trap for her—and she really couldn't be mad about it. Yes, some women would look at his actions as creepy, stalker-like even, but she'd never once felt the ominous fear that usually came with being watched by a malevolent person. And, he hadn't actually said he'd been watching her, only that he'd been slavering after her—for two years! Dear God! That man—the one who looked like sex incarnate—had seen her and wanted her, had even chased her and captured her. All because of one moment in a courtroom.

If that wasn't flattering, she couldn't think of anything that was.

She'd never been deluded about herself; she knew she wasn't what most men wanted. She wasn't a size 6 with a tiny waist, a thigh gap, and a manageable set of tits. She was extra in all the wrong places, and had—for years—hidden behind loose-fitting clothes, bulky jackets, and a snarky attitude. It wasn't until she'd entered law school and seen the plethora of professional women—all shapes, sizes, and colors—making a killing in the courtroom that she'd realized her true potential. Her confidence had taken a 90-degree upturn, and she'd started buying the fitted skirts, the cleavage bearing tops, and the flirty shoes. Despite that, she hadn't allowed herself to believe that any man would find her attractive enough to want to have sex with her.

And now she knew...*this* one did. This drop dead sexy man wanted her—had wanted her since seeing her the first time. The thought sent tremors of excitement into her core.

As he spoke in monosyllabic mumbles, he watched her, his gaze roving over her, and her body felt his invisible touch. With a final word in Russian, he hung up the phone, still not looking away from her.

"Well," he began, "it appears my ability to anticipate my woman's needs has only gotten better." A wolfish, sexy smile lifted one corner of his mouth, and her heart thudded at the picture he presented—hungry animal, preparing to appease his appetite.

And I'll get to appease mine as well.

Straightening, she unclasped her hands and leaned back into the couch, crossing her legs in a manner she knew would tease him; her skirt rode up her thighs, showing glimpses of her caramel skin.

"And...how have you anticipated my needs? How do you even know what I need?" she asked, her voice a throaty murmur. *God, what am I doing teasing him?* She was totally out of her element. She would need years of expertise to handle this man. And she only had from now until their wedding in what, two, three days?

"One look at you and I knew I couldn't wait to marry you," he drawled, his gaze dropping to her mouth.

Anxiety and excitement crashed into her chest, making her breath catch. "What do you mean?" Why did she sound so sleep-rumpled?

He stopped, just in front of the couch, his shins brushing against her knees. She looked up at him, not allowing herself to be cowed by how much she wanted him, and he looked right back, unblinking.

"I had Gregor call the priest. He is on his way up." His smile lit up the room, and subsequently lit her up, too. "We will be married within the next half hour."

Half. Hour. Half hour. Half hour! *Omigod, omigod, omigod! Madre di Dios, Madre di Dios—Hell, the man has me swearing in Spanish!* Unable to wrap her mind around what he'd just said, so easily, like he'd just told her he ordered the chicken instead of the fish, she shot to her feet. She needed to be doing something other than sitting; she needed to be moving, ridding herself of the nervous and sexual energies that were pumping through her.

Before she could settle her mind and slow her heart, the elevator dinged, and she stopped breathing. A man of about eighty stepped from the car, followed by the dour-faced Gregor. The man, apparently the priest, was wearing a black suit coat, a white button down, and a collar.

Vitali turned away from her to greet the newcomer.

"Father Itszack, welcome," he said warmly. "I am so glad you could come at such short notice."

The short yet reed-thin man beamed a warm smile in return. "Anything for you, my son. To think, Vitali Pavlovich finally settling down..." Father Itszack's bright brown gaze landed on Mariana. And instead of feeling uncomfortable at the prospect of him performing her wedding to a near stranger, she was strangely comforted. Like if this man could trust Vitali, so could Mariana. It bolstered her decision to go through with the ceremony—rushed as it was.

I hope my trust isn't misplaced... The slinking, slithering voice of doubt whispered in her mind.

Vitali grinned at Father Itszack. "Believe me, Father, I am *not* settling," he drawled, turning to pour heat into Mariana, the green of his eyes burning with an unholy fire. She fought off a full-body tremble, and forcing herself to turn from Vitali, she offered the older man a smile. Reaching out, he took her hand in his, patting it like any old priest would. How adorable.

"I can see what you mean, Vitali. She is breathtaking," Father Itszack announced, and Vitali grunted.

"You're damn right she is," Vitali replied and, unthinkingly, Mariana turned and slapped Vitali on the arm, shocked at his language in front of a man of God. Too late, she realized what she'd done; she'd struck her fiancé. As her stomach bottomed out, she peered up at Vitali from beneath her lashes, terror mixing with trepidation writhing within her. But in a flash, they were replaced with chagrin.

Vitali was grinning at her, that lopsided sexy as hell grin that sent her heart spinning, turning her panties into liquid cotton.

"She has fire! I like her!" Father Itszack said, then chuckled, and Mariana's cheeks burned with mortification.

His eyes watching her every expression, Vitali chucked, too, the deep timbre of it rumbling through her chest—and straight to her pussy. She was wet and there was a priest there, for God's sake! A new flush flew up her neck and into her face.

Nearly groaning at the awkwardness of her predicament, she almost missed it when Vitali said, "We're ready, aren't we, Mariana...?"

At the sound of her name, her brain stalled, but then kicked into high gear at the look of curious wisdom in the priest's eyes.

Not trusting her voice just yet, Mariana nodded, offering Vitali a strangled smile.

"Good." Father Itszack pulled a deep purple and white stole from his leather bag, looped it around his neck, and then retrieved a small black leather book.

With a single nod to Gregor, Vitali summoned the man from the corner. He came forward holding a small Tiffany Blue box. Vitali took the box and turned to her, pulling the lid open to reveal a ring with the largest diamond she'd ever laid eyes on. The setting was a princess cut, and the band was encrusted with eight smaller diamonds. The diamond in the crown of the ring glittered and glinted as the lights from overhead hit it.

She sucked in a breath, numbed by the sheer size of the ring. With a diamond that size, she'd be well and truly claimed by Vitali. As his wife. Like a carbon billboard on her finger.

Mariana didn't know how to feel about that. The man was certainly putting "a ring on it".

Vitali reached down and took her hand in his, gripping it tightly, the surprisingly rough skin of his palms seemed to caress the soft flesh of hers. Rough yet gentle. Strong yet soft.

Mariana Sanchez, brassy, bold attorney, turned to living fire at his touch. Images of that same hot, strong hand, trailing, feather light, over her sensitized body nearly made her knees give out.

"All right, then. Let's get started..."

Father Itszack's voice disappeared behind the roar of emotions in her head. She listened to the words of the ceremony as if in a bubble, but when the priest turned to her, indicating she recite her vows, everything became clear. She was getting married. She was finally taking that step—the one step she thought impossible, sitting behind her big desk in her big office watching life flash by. It was her chance for a piece of happiness, and she was going to take it by the throat.

Swallowing down the sudden rush of tears, she let the fear fall away. Smiling up into Vitali's handsome face, she declared, "I, Mariana Louisa, take you Vitali..."

8

She was stunning...and she was *his*; the large and expensive wedding ring on her finger said that. Pride burst through his chest. His ring on her finger was a proclamation, a contract made of precious jewels. No man would ever have what he'd claimed as his own.

Vitali sat across from Mrs. Pavlovich and watched as she talked with their companion, her hands flying with excitement, her eyes alight. Her cheeks were flushed, her mouth often split into a cock-teasing grin, and her husky voice, when filled with passion, was like a death knell to his self-control. He had to get her alone.

The ceremony had taken only ten minutes, but he'd invited Father Itszack to stay for dinner, which was a comfortable affair, with delicious food, fine wine, and brilliant conversation. The priest had asked Mariana about her life in Chicago, and the woman had glowed, pouring out her love for her career, her family, and her friends—it was truly beautiful. *And she was his.*

"Gregor," Vitali called to the man standing like a shadow beside the elevator door. "Please escort Father Itszack to the car." Gregor nodded, Father Itszack shook Vitali's hand, bid good evening—and good luck—to Mariana, and then left with a nearly silent *whoosh* of the elevator doors closing.

And then they were alone.

He and his wife.

The room seemed to vibrate with the pounding of his heart against his ribs... He'd waited so long for her, and now...

"My wife..." he held the last word out, savoring the sound of it on his tongue, and the sight of Mariana shuddering, her flushed skin inviting his hands to come touch. Her slightly parted lips beckoning him to come taste. The sparks of desire in her cocoa eyes begging him to make the first move... And so he would.

"I hope the ceremony was to your liking. I know you want another, American, ceremony as well." He walked toward her, slowly, allowing her gaze to flutter over him as he moved, the appreciation written in her expression made his balls ache. And when her gaze finally landed on the noticeable bulge in his pants, her eyes widened, but then narrowed, her nostrils flaring.

Hmmm...his wife liked what she saw—his obvious desire for her in return.

"Mariana," he drawled, coming to stand before her, her eyes flying from his crotch to meet his gaze. "Are you pleased?" Her pleasure mattered more to him than he ever thought possible; pleasing her, in all ways, had suddenly become his mission. His obsession.

Her black eyelashes fluttered, as if fanning the flames of the blush that pinkened her cheeks.

How far does that blush go...will her pussy be just as pink?

She cleared her throat, pushing herself to standing, and clasping her hands in front of herself demurely.

"I was satisfied by the efficiency of the ceremony," she said, her husky voice wreaking havoc on his blood.

He cocked a grin, pouring every wicked intention into it. "That isn't what I meant, *tol'ko moya*, and you know it."

"I know what you meant," she retorted. "I just didn't want to make it that easy for you."

At the flicker of challenge in her eyes, he let loose a chuckle. "Defiant, fiery... I like that," he drawled, stepping closer to drag his finger from just below her ear, down her neck and collar bone, and right over the velvet soft globe of her left breast.

"Exquisite," he murmured, in awe of the silkiness and heat of her flesh.

She trembled, her breath catching. "You have to stop doing that. I can't think when you do that..."

Raising a single eyebrow, he did it again, his own defiance coming to the fore. Fire against fire. This time, he dragged his finger from the top of one breast to the other, and watched as she watched his hand, her eyes heavy-lidded.

She liked it, liked having her husband's finger sliding over her inviting flesh. Flesh that was, even now, prickling with tiny goosebumps. Her body's response to his focused attention was a revelation. He must have more.

"No...I don't think I will stop doing that. I think I will do much more...wife." Again, the word on his tongue sent liquid fire through his blood. He couldn't help but marvel at her—this amazing, sexy, fierce, compassionate, and intelligent woman was now his wife. His *dusha*...soul in human form. The one he would share the rest of his life with...

One day at a time. One night *at a time...* This night. Their wedding night.

Drawing her into his arms, he reveled in the feel of her curves against his hardness. Though she was petite and he was large, they fit together as if Fate had designed them, one for the other. Part of him—the cynical part that had been honed from years of scraping and clawing in the orphanage —said that he was being foolish, that Fate was a fickle bitch that cared nothing for him or Mariana. But...looking down at his wife now, feeling her against him, smelling the scent of roses wafting from that sensitive place, just below her ear, he wanted to believe in Fate.

"What?" Mariana asked, her brows pinched. "What are you thinking about that has you looking so...pensive?"

Perceptive. And ballsy. God she was going to be a fun package to unwrap.

While she was good at perceiving his change in mood, he wasn't quite ready to explain it. He could barely figure it out himself. When had he become a moon-eyed romantic fool? Slamming the door on those flowery thoughts of Fate and being made for one another, Vitali cupped Mariana's face with his hands. Her eyes widened.

"I don't want to talk about it right now." To prove his point, he leaned down and brushed his lips over hers—ever so slightly, like a feather along her mouth. "I would much rather talk about getting you out of that incredible skirt, pulling that sweater up over your head, and peeling your bra and panties from your body so I can see every inch of you. And once we're done *talking*...we can start...*not* talking," he drawled low, his voice husky with unspent lust.

"That sounds amazing," she purred, her cheeks flushed, her eyes bright. "But—"

He slid his thumbs over her mouth to silence her naysaying. "But nothing. I know you seem to think you will disappointment me, but there's something you need to know, wife."

He moved his thumbs so she could speak. "What's that?" she breathed.

"I have been dreaming about this moment for two years—that's 730 days—and the only way you could disappoint me is if you don't kiss me right now."

He held his breath, his body tense with waiting, wanting, anticipating her response. Would she...?

At the catch in her breathing, he smiled.

She smiled back. Oooo, he liked it when she smiled like that...

GROWING EVER MORE COURAGEOUS, MARIANA REACHED UP TO wind her arms around his neck, and touched her lips to his. After a moment, during which the world stopped turning, Vitali plunged in, taking control of the kiss, teasing her mouth open with the tip of his eager tongue, and then teasing her tongue to come and play with his. Sucking the air from her lungs, Vitali made her think of nothing else but sucking his air into hers—until she had no idea whose breath was whose. She didn't care. He was kissing her like she was the most delicious thing he'd ever tasted, and dear God in heaven, he was certainly the most delicious thing she'd ever tasted. A mix like whiskey—sweet on the tip of the tongue but burning on the way down.

Then his lips were searing a path from her mouth, down her neck, leaving a trail of hypersensitive goosebumps in his wake. The sensations firing through her made her nipples ache, the feeling of his chest rubbing against them was exquisite in its pleasure and pain—like an edgy ecstasy she wanted to bury herself in.

"God, Mariana, *tol'ko moya*," he rumbled into her neck, making her tremble, "I need to see you, to see what this sexy outfit is hiding from me."

Pulling away, she dropped her hands from his chest and took hold of the bottom of her sweater, her heart racing. This was it, the moment of truth. She'd never bared herself to any man, and to do so now, in front of the sexiest man on earth, was both terrifying and exhilarating. Steeling her resolve, she began pulling the sweater up, and Vitali's darkened gaze watched her every movement with rapt hunger.

She fought the urge to hurry it up and get the unveiling over with, because there was something in her that wanted to tease him, make him truly ravenous for her. It was her first time, but it wasn't his, and she wanted to make their first time together one she would always remember. One he would always remember above all others.

By the time she got the sweater above her belly button, Vitali's breathing was labored, like he'd run a marathon, and her blood was pounding in her ears. Closing her eyes against the expression she feared seeing, she wrenched the sweater up and over her head, dropping it at her feet.

She held her breath, and when Vitali didn't say anything, she peeked through her lashes at him.

The look of awe and unfettered desire on his face made her pussy clench and her skin sing.

"You are perfect," he whispered heavily before reaching out to cup one swollen breast in his large hand. She shuddered, and he rubbed a thumb over her nipple, making her drag in a breath on a hiss. "Even your response to me if perfect." He kissed her again, and while his mouth was busy turning her mind to mush, his other hand reached up to cup her other breast. She groaned, he growled then tweaked a nipple with his thumb and forefinger. She gasped, which gave him even greater access to her mouth.

Breaking their kiss, Vitali bent his head and took a nipple into his mouth through the fabric of her bra. Lights burst behind her eyes—she'd never felt anything so amazing.

"Ah! Vitali," she cried, nearly going limp. Instinctively, she held his head to her breast, arching into him, silently begging him to take more, give her more.

He sucked the aching point, pulling it deeper into his scorching mouth. His tongue twirled around it, flicking it. Then, he did the same to her other nipple.

With her mind occupied with what he was doing to her tits, she barely realized it when he began sliding his hand down her quivering belly to slide it into the waistband of her skirt. She'd never felt a man's hand there before—it was totally new, but she discovered she really liked it. And when Vitali's hand skimmed over the apex of her sex, she shuddered, her whole body going up in flames.

"Oh, Mariana, you are so lush, so beautiful—look at you, you're coming apart and I haven't been inside you yet."

At the thought of him inside her, a sensation like crackling energy and burning lava danced through her veins.

9

Vitali had never known such heady desire in his life. He'd fucked his share of women, but none had brought him this close to coming without being naked. Mariana was amazing, her cheeks flushed, her lips swollen from his kisses, her chocolate eyes melting—she was truly gorgeous.

Desperate to touch more of her, and to have her touch him, he put enough distance between them to rip his own shirt from his body, sending buttons flying. She had to have sensed his intentions because she reached behind her and unfastened the hooks of her bra, but before it could fall and reveal her glorious breasts to him, she clasped the fabric to her chest.

She averted her gaze, biting her lip in a show of nervousness.

"Mariana, *tol'ko moya*, I have wanted to see you naked before me for two years. Please do not deny me the pleasure now."

Her flush deepened but she let the fabric fall, uncovering two beautiful breasts. Large, round, a soft brown with dark pink nipples—his cock throbbed at the sight of them.

He scrubbed his hand over his face and smacked his lips. "Fuck, Mariana... Those are just fucking perfect." And to prove he meant it, he stepped forward, cupped her breasts in his hands, and took her nipple into his mouth again, savoring the salty taste of her flesh on his tongue. When she groaned, pushing her breast into his face, he reveled in the pleasure he was giving her.

His hand returned to her waistband, unzipping the skirt at the side, and pushing it down until the skin-tight skirt was trapped around her lower thighs. He slid his hand over the flesh of her hips and thighs, relishing the warmth and softness, wondering what it would feel like to have that warmth and softness wrapped around his waist as he pounded into her.

Again, his cock throbbed, tired of all the promises without any of the follow through. With one last push, he sent the skirt to the floor beside the other clothes. He pulled away to stare down at her panties. The light purple fabric was dark purple at her pussy.

"Fuck, you're wet for me," he growled then cupped her sex, sliding a finger along her folds. Mariana moaned, and he captured the sound with his mouth, kissing her with all the pent-up desire he was barely able to contain.

Another moan escaped her lips. "You make me this way, Vitali, and I don't know what the hell is going on."

He chuckled. "That is what we call mindless with desire—you're mindless for me, Mariana."

She sucked in a breath and leaned into him, pressing her naked breasts against his chest.

“If that’s the case, get those pants off and show me what it truly means to be fucked.”

Her words made his heart halt, the sudden wrenching stealing the heat from his blood for a moment. Fuck her...? That didn’t seem right. It didn’t feel like he was fucking her... It felt like he was cherishing her, adoring her...making love to her.

Dammit.

As if to prove himself wrong, he bent and picked Mariana up, throwing her lusciousness over his shoulder. She squealed and smacked his back.

“Vitali! Put me down! I’m going to break you in half!” she yelled, but he paid no heed. He felt like a caveman, born of ice, carrying his prey into his den, where he would devour her, piece by piece by piece. He carried her into the spacious bedroom, where a large bed sat on a dais facing the windows which were overlooking the city.

A sense of pride filled his chest. He was going to claim his woman in front of all the heartless fuckers in Moscow, the same people who said he’d never amount to anything. The same people who told him he was nothing but a whore’s son, a man who would never know the true warmth of a good woman.

Fuck them. He would prove them wrong, and he’d have one hell of a good time doing it.

With great care, Vitali bent and let Mariana slide from his shoulder and onto the bed. She looked delectable, like a treat waiting to be sampled.

She read his mind, she had to have that power, because she cocked a most seductive smile and lay back on the bed, her arms splayed over the crème-colored silk sheets. The flush that had begun on her cheeks covered the rest of her, and he'd be a dead man if he didn't see what color her pussy was —would it be the same lush pink?

Kneeling on the bed, still wearing his pants, he shot back to his feet, fumbling with his belt buckle to get one of the last barriers between his cock and her cunny out of the way. It took him more time than usual, because he was so goddamn eager, but once he had his pants undone, he pushed them down. Not surprisingly, his trousers and boxer briefs caught on his engorged penis, and Mariana's gaze landed just there in that moment. Her smoky brown eyes grew wide, and her lips parted on a gasp, and her flush deepened.

And his cock loved the attention—throbbing painfully.

He pushed once more, dislodging his clothing and revealing the whole of him to his wife's starving eyes.

"Hell, Vitali... I'm not going to act like a total idiot and say you won't fit, but please, don't make it hurt...too much..."

Vitali, heart pounding, blood surging into his groin, looked down at his penis. It was long—9 inches—and thick, so thick some lovers couldn't get their mouths around it. But he'd bet his fortune Mariana could.

The image of Mariana swallowing his cock made precum gather at his tip.

Shit! If he didn't get inside her soon, he'd spend on her belly—like a fucking teenager.

"I'll make it good, I promise," he declared then pressed his nose into the flesh of her belly. It was soft, warm—just like Mariana—and he inhaled her scent. She smelled of arousal, the subtle scent of woman.

Delicious.

Hooking his fingers around the thin band of her panties, he ripped the damned things into pieces, finally revealing the treasure they were hiding. A pillowy bush of dark brown hair was trimmed into a narrow runway that led straight down to paradise. Trembling with his own need, he planted his nose right there at her mons, inhaling the headiness of her womanhood. His head swam.

"God, you smell like heaven, Mariana," he said, his voice gravelly.

"Vitali, you need to stop playing around and fuck me!" Mariana cried, her eyes wild, her hair spread out over the blanket, her legs open wide in invitation. "If you don't take me I just might lose my goddamn mind."

Who was he to deny his wife what she wanted? Growling, he climbed over her and kissed her lips, plundering the heat and sweetness of her mouth. With one hand he cupped her breast, playing with the hard pebble of her nipple, and with his other hand, he spread her legs wider to allow for his hips to wedge in there good and tight.

And then his cock was at her entrance, and his body sang with the anticipation, two years heavy.

Shuddering, forcing his mind to focus, he stared down at her beneath him, and sucked in a breath to steady himself.

"Are you ready? Because if you aren't, tell me now, because once I start, it's going to take a fucking firing squad to make me stop," he growled.

A low, sexy chuckle made her tits shake. "Oh, I'm more than ready, Vitali. I will die if you don't put that in me right, the fuck, now!"

On her command, he pushed inside her narrow channel, the tightness strangling a cry from his chest.

In that second, the desire to protect her overrode his desire to be in her. "What about protection?"

She grunted and slid her hands up his arms to grip his shoulders. "I got a shot—no worries for another five years."

That was good enough for him. He wasn't about to share Mariana, even if his babies would be gorgeous.

"Damn, baby, I'm going to explode before I even get it all in."

She tensed. "I will kill you if you do!" She braced her hands against his chest.

"God, Vitali, I need this..." A keening cry escaped her lips, and she thrashed her head. Good, she was as delirious as he was.

He pushed in further, just enough to feel a little resistance. She tensed again.

She held her breath for a moment, then let it out slowly.

"You okay?" he asked, determined to ease her pain so she could experience the pleasure.

She nodded. "I'm good."

With a grunt and a practiced thrust, he seated himself fully inside his wife. Blinding lights gathered behind his eyes; she was so hot, so tight, like a sheath snuggly fitted to a sword. *His* sword.

She was made for him.

With more strength than he thought he owned, he held still, waiting for her body to grow accustomed to the fullness, to the intrusion. Once her body loosened around him, he pulled out slowly, then pushed in slowly.

Her soft and surprised moan lit him on fire; he pulled out again, thrusting into her with more force. And he did it again, fully seating himself within her welcoming, clenching heat.

"Vitali, ooh, *Vitali*, that feels so good!" Mariana cried out, lifting her hips to meet his thrusts. God, he loved his wife's bold passion. She stoked him, like a blaze caught at dry timbers. He would lose control if he didn't check himself.

This was her first time, she deserved her pleasure, and he deserved to give it to her. Bending down, her kissed her, his tongue matching the motion of his own hips, thrusting and moving in slow circles. Breaking the kiss to breathe, Vitali then bent his head to her breast, flicking the tip with his tongue. First one breast, then other.

Mariana arched up with her chest, and then pushed up with her hips, her movements like an undulating wave, crashing into the shore.

He thrust into her, angling his movements to grind against her sensitive clit.

And then her tight, wet, hot channel was flexing, contracting —her orgasm was building.

Lost, broken, in need of his own release, he rocked into her, deep, hard. The sound of his body slamming into hers rang in his ears; music he never wanted to turn down.

Racing to meet her in the explosion of pleasure, Vitali braced his hands on either side of Mariana's head, allowing his weight to aid in his thrusts—ever deeper, ever harder, ever faster. Panting, sweat dripping from his brow onto Mariana's bouncing breasts, Vitali was on fire, his body screaming for the ultimate moment—

The earth shifted, the sky fell, the fabric of the universe tore asunder, and his orgasm ripped through him. Throwing his head back, he bellowed his pleasure into the heavens. And Mariana screamed her release, her sheath spasming wildly, her body stiffening and then falling back into the bed, her arms spread wide, her chest heaving, her eyes wide and pinned to his face.

And what he saw there made him question everything.

Despite her brain's insistence that she was sore and tired, her body was willing to take more of Vitali, his ravenous mouth, his thick cock, and all the orgasms he'd given her.

Six. The man had given her six orgasms—and it wasn't even morning yet!

"God, Vitali, I don't know if I'm going to survive until breakfast," she purred into his chest then stretched her arms out over his abs—the taut muscles flexing as he clenched them. The black hairs on his pecs tickled her nostrils and cheeks.

It was strange how intimate that seemed.

"Are you *that* spent, wife?" he asked, his deep voice rumbling straight into her head.

She groaned, both ready for round seven and still sore from rounds one through six.

"Yes—but that's not what I was talking about." She slid her hand up to rest it over his heart, which was beating a heavy yet steady rhythm. "I meant that I am going to starve to death before then. All this *talking* has burned off the few bites I had for dinner."

He chuckled. God, he sounded sexy when he chuckled—hell, the man would be sexy reading the back of a cereal box. There was something panty-melting about a man with an accent, and Russian had always been one of her favorites. She'd even taken Russian in high school, because she already knew Spanish. And while she wasn't all that fluent or even proficient in Vitali's language, she wanted to make him happy. So, once she settled in to her new life in Moscow, she'd look into getting private language lessons. Perhaps she'd surprise him during their second wedding ceremony.

With a moan, Vitali shifted beneath her, and she could see the outline of his erection through the thin silk sheet.

"I know what you're thinking," he said, tilting her face up to meet his gaze. "And you're right, I do want to make you scream my name again." Heat blasted through her, coming to set fire to her core. "But...my wife is hungry, so I must feed her."

Laughing, Mariana slid from the bed, dressed in a seriously comfortable robe Vitali laid out for her, and followed her sexy as hell—and still naked—husband down the hall to the living area.

"I'll have the kitchen send up...what? Waffles? Eggs? Bacon?"

She nodded, her stomach choosing that moment to growl. This time, heat blasted through her face.

Vitali grinned at her. "Everything it is."

Watching him as he headed to the phone to call for breakfast at 4 A.M., Mariana was struck by a heady realization. She was married. She was this man's wife. And she'd just had the most amazing sex. What a way to lose her virginity.

Damn! I can't wait to tell Mia... The guilt that usually surfaced at the thought of the friend she'd lied to didn't roll in as she thought it would. It wasn't as though she'd lied to hurt her —it was legally required lying. She couldn't tell anyone about Diamond Bridal Agency and her contract for marriage. Sworn to secrecy.

Suddenly, she was excited about the prospect of going back to America. Facing Mia, Mia's anger at Mariana's secrets, and the responsibilities of her law practice didn't seem so overwhelming as they had the day before. She wasn't alone anymore...

10

Two days since their rushed wedding. Two days of mind-blowing sex. Two days of putting off the real world so he could simply enjoy the delights of his wife.

But now, real life was calling. Literally.

Grasping his cell phone in his hand, he listened to his VP of Sales ramble on about some shit in Malaysia, and how none of the corporate heads wanted to talk to Lyuba. "Dammit, Milos," he growled in Russian as he peered at Mariana who was watching him from over the rim of her coffee mug. "I told you I need at least of week of uninterrupted time. It's my honeymoon for fuck's sake!"

"Yeah, but they don't know that. And even if they did, they probably would say the same thing." Milos let out a slow, heavy breath. "Lyuba is kicking up a lot of hornets. She actually pulled the Donovan Innovations deal because the guy refused to take her to dinner."

Anger bled into his voice. In Russian, he blurted, "The hell you say!" Casting a quick glance to Mariana, he noticed that she'd flinched—more than likely at the tone and volume of his voice.

"The guy is married, Vitali. But that didn't matter to her. She is on a rampage—and I think you know why."

He might.

"Did anyone tell her about my business in Moscow? I left strict instructions to keep her out of it. I didn't want to deal with her drama while I was getting to know Mariana." The truth was, he should have fired Lyuba years ago, but...well, he'd let his guilt over their breakup sway his decision.

Damn his guilt. And damn Lyuba for putting him in this position.

"Shit," he barked, already feeling the tension robbing him of his bliss—bliss Mariana had brought with her body, her laughter, and her—just her.

Just then, a heavy, familiar voice slithered in his head; "*You're pussy-whipped, Vitali. What kind of man lets a woman rule him for two years and then sinks her claws into him once he's had a taste of her sex?*" A man like him, apparently.

Tired of the whirling, clashing, upheaval of disparate emotions, he steeled his resolve to put his business ahead of his cock. "Fine. I'll meet you in Kuala Lumpur in 12 hours."

"Right," Milos responded then ended their call. Never one for small talk, that Milos.

Preparing himself to turn to his wife and tell her their honeymoon was cut short by the antics of his ex-lover, Vitali spun on his heel and flashed a smile he hoped would allay any of the anxiety she may had felt during his phone conversation.

"What was that about?" she asked, eyeing him with curiosity mixed with a hint of...jealousy? Where the hell did that come from? He'd spoken in Russian.

Settling back into his seat at the table where he'd been enjoying an omelet before his cell rang and he excused himself to chew Milos out, he stared down at the now cold food.

Grunting, he pushed his plate to the middle of the table and grabbed his mug of coffee. Also cold. Well, damn. He had to fly to Malaysia on an empty stomach.

"That was my VP. He says there is trouble with an acquisition in Asia and that I need to come straighten it out in person." He rolled his shoulders, tension roiling through his body at the flicker of disappointment clouding her eyes.

An invisible hand punched him in the gut. He rubbed his belly, trying to rid himself of the uncomfortable sensation of failing at something. No matter how small it was. Yeah, he was disappointed, too. Of all the women he'd seduced, dated, and fucked, Mariana was—by far—the most amazing of them all. She was different, and not because she was his wife. There was something about her that put all the other faceless women out of his mind. She was everything he'd never thought to have wrapped up in a spicy, curvy package.

"So...you're leaving," she said flatly. She put the mug down on the table and made to push away and stand. "I suppose I can find something to do with myself while you're gone." From the strain in her voice, he could tell that she didn't want to stay, but he didn't want her to stay, either. She stood up and attempted to hide her pinched expression by turning away.

Nyet! She would not hide from him. He couldn't make her happy if she hid her unhappiness from him. *Why does her happiness matter? You've finally gotten her, and now that you've slaked two years of lust, you can put her aside and do whatever the hell you want. Make* you *happy, Vitali.* Because no one else gave a fuck about him.

But...he *hadn't* slaked his lust yet. Not by a long shot.

"You're coming with me." He shot to his feet, coming around their small breakfast table in two strides. In a flash, she was pressed against him, her face tipped up to receive his kiss. It was muscle memory with her. She just knew—by instinct—that he needed to kiss her. He devoured her lips, his tongue lashing against her in a feverish demand for more, and she gave it. Her passion was intoxicating, like a drug he never wanted to kick.

Careful...

With strength drawn up from his heels, he broke the kiss. Breath heaving, he continued. "We are still on our honeymoon, wife. Just because business demands my presence in Malaysia doesn't mean *you* can't have me as well," Vitali cooed, wiggling his eyebrows.

Her burst of laughter was well worth looking like an idiot.

"I see," she said between giggles. "I guess I'd better go pack, then." She sobered immediately, a wariness and uncertainty chilling her once warm gaze. "How long will we be in Malaysia?"

"However long it takes to finish the business, then we will come back here," he replied, planting his hands on his hips —a defensive gesture he'd picked up at St. Maria's Orphanage, where looking big, bad, and unintimidated kept you from losing your meal portion.

Mariana stepped back and he immediately felt the loss of her heat, her calming yet arousing presence.

"Why?" And why did he suddenly want to pull away, guarding himself against attack?

As if reading his mind, she stiffened. "The contract stipulates that we have a follow-up marriage ceremony in America, to make this legal in the U.S."

Running his fingers through his hair, he allowed the anxiety in his chest to spread outward. "*Blyad*," he cursed, then reached for her, determined to rescue the intimate moment they'd had only moments before. "We will." He pulled her into him, grabbing her hips and grinding his quickly growing erection into her belly. His mind wanted him to withdrawal to regroup and figure out why this little slip of a woman could make him crash against the rocks so violently. But his body...it wanted to plunge inside her, feel her clenching around him, hear her scream his name as she came.

Use your brain, Vitali. Never have you allowed anyone to distract you from what needed to be done. He needed to get to Malaysia and keep Lyuba from tanking his business deal. That meant putting Mariana out of his mind and telling his body to calm the hell down.

Grumbling to himself, he dropped his hands and stepped away from the oh so delectable woman.

"Go. Pack. We leave in an hour," he said, offering her a smile to offset the sharpness in his tone. She narrowed her eyes at him, at once wary again.

Dammit.

"Fine." She shrugged then turned and stalked toward the bedroom, disappearing into the room where he'd made love to her no more than an hour ago. He pinched the bridge of his nose, a headache building behind his eyes. He had to stop doing that; thinking about Mariana, her luscious body, and all the things he wanted to do to it. *Da,* he'd wanted to marry her and have her in his bed, but he hadn't really considered what actually having her would mean. It meant a constant hard-on, a loss of focus, and the sinking feeling that perhaps he was falling into a trap of some kind.

Shaking himself, he followed after her, determined to pack for the trip and put orgasming with Mariana from his mind —at least long enough to fire Lyuba and fix yet another problem in his company.

11

It was her first trip to Malaysia. She should be excited, filled with the thrill of discovering and experiencing a new place and culture. But she wasn't. She could only watch her husband tip-tapping away at the keys on his laptop, doing whatever business needed to be done before they landed. And ignoring her.

With nothing more than a simple nod since taking off, Vitali had completely put her from his mind. Her—his wife. The woman he'd fucked into oblivion that morning. The woman who couldn't stop thinking about him, about putting her lips around his cock and making him groan. The woman who was pissed as hell about whoever the hell Lyuba was.

No, she didn't speak fluent Russian, but she didn't need to speak Russian to know that some woman named Lyuba was causing problems in Vitali's business deal. And, from the tone of Vitali's voice, and his carefully chosen words, Mariana would be a fool to think that there wasn't something between her husband and this woman.

Petya appeared, dressed smartly in her uniform and name tag, handing her a glass of Captain Morgan and Coke, one of her favorite drinks. Mariana sipped it. It tasted like a big, fat burning nothing on her tongue. Jealousy made everything taste like shit. She should know—for years she'd let jealousy fuel her drive to succeed. She wanted what the white couple in the front pew of the church had—the big house, the fancy cars, the tailored clothes. They always looked so happy, always filled with whatever Mariana, the chubby, Latina didn't have. And so, she worked her ass off in school, earned her law degree, passed the bar, got a job as a public defender, and then kicked serious ass in the higher profile cases. Finally...she was sitting at the top, in her 2,000 square-foot office, wearing her fancy clothes, looking at the keys to that fancy car... And it all felt meaningless. It took something Mia had said in passing to start the downward spiral that had led her to this moment.

"Got a man to share that brand-new bed of yours? Looks kind of empty..."

Mariana had recoiled—and not because of what Mia had said, but rather the truth that had pealed through her skull. That next morning, her penthouse apartment no longer looked like the luxurious prize she'd earned. It looked like the tomb she'd be buried in.

Vitali's cell rang, pulling Mariana out of her self-imposed mind-fuck. Who was calling?

Shit. Back to the jealousy. The nausea, the chest pains, the uneasy feeling—yeah, jealousy sucked ass—as Mia would say.

And she had no reason to be jealous, not really. She'd only met Vitali three days ago. Yes, they were married, but she had no idea what kind of man she married. That's one of the major downsides to marrying a complete stranger based on an application supplied to a bridal agency. Vitali could be a womanizing sleaze bag for all she knew. He could have lied about seeing her and wanting her from the very first moment. All of the bedroom acrobatics could have just been him blowing off some steam. She was a fool to think that a man like Vitali would be satisfied with a woman, inexperienced and far from the super model beauties a man like Vitali could get with a snap of his fingers. He could very well plan to keep some on the side for when he got bored with his plus-sized ball-n-chain.

Placing the unfinished drink on the table beside her, she let her gaze roam the cabin. She was in the same private jet she'd arrived in, but this time around, the cabin felt smaller, more suffocating. It was hard to breathe without inhaling the scent of musk and manhood that was Vitali's signature scent. It was a heady scent that could make her drunk if she let it. And she wouldn't. She was a strong, professional woman, a woman who had never let men come between her and what she wanted, and what she wanted right now was her husband's undivided attention.

Still on his cell, Mariana knew she couldn't just start talking to him, so, she did the next best thing; she unbuckled herself, unbuttoned her sporty black suit coat, and slowly slid it from her shoulders—the whole time, her gaze was riveted to Vitali.

As if sensing her intent, he looked up from his laptop screen for the first time, his gaze flying from her overheated, flushed face to where her hand was poised over the first button in her blouse.

Time to begin the show.

Taking a deep breath to fortify her nerves, she slipped the first button from its hole. Then the next. By the time she'd reached half way down, she could feel the tension wafting from Vitali, and the burning, hotter than lava gaze in his emerald eyes could scorch her...if she weren't already on fire.

With a flick of his wrist, Vitali closed the lid to his laptop. In the next second, he hung up on whoever it was he was speaking with, and then stowed his cell phone in the pocket beside his seat. The man looked like a starving wolf, his entire face taut, nostrils flared, and lips pulled back from his teeth in a show of predatory menace.

Was it wrong that she liked him like that, that she liked him possessive, hungry—like an alpha beast zeroing in on his prey?

As if sensing their need for privacy, Petya entered the cockpit and closed the door behind her. Vitali unbuckled.

Mariana held her breath and watched, enraptured, as he extended his arm, flipped his hand over, and gestured for her to come to him. A single finger held all the power in the world in that moment.

Since when did you allow any man to beckon you? Since she began falling under his spell, that's when! Still... Somewhat annoyed at his alpha bullshit she nearly scoffed at him and returned the motion—with a totally different finger. But she needed this, she needed *him*...and he was finally looking at her. Finally focusing on *her*. And that alone was empowering.

Maybe he's actually putting business—and Lyuba—out of his mind.

Holding her breath, she slowly stood, then kicked her heels from her feet. Though the pilot was keeping the plane level, she felt as though she were walking through turbulence. Once she was standing before Vitali, staring down into his now dark green eyes, she realized her mistake: she thought she could tease the beast without consequences, but from the look of ravenous desire on his face, she knew she'd delivered herself up to be devoured.

12

Her body still singing from the amazing sex in the jet seat, Mariana didn't really mind that Vitali ordered dinner to their room in the sky-high penthouse suite in the hotel in Kuala Lumpur. Every nerve hummed, every blood vein sang, and her heart couldn't stop lurching every time she thought about riding Vitali's cock while he nibbled her breasts.

Never in her life did she think she would join the Mile-High Club. She hid a grin and swallowed a giggle at the thought. Vitali chose that moment to stalk back into their bedroom after conferring with their personal butler about where they wanted dinner.

"I asked them to put the meal on the terrace," he said without preamble, his expression about as empty as her stomach. "I figured that since this is your first time in Malaysia, you'd enjoy eating while looking out over the city." He pulled off his coat and tossed it over the foot of the bed—it was both intimate and robotic.

His thoughtfulness warmed her, and she smiled. "Thank you. That sounds wonderful."

He returned her smile, but his expression remained guarded. Her excitement about sharing a meal with her husband and experiencing Malaysia for the first time with him died in a blink. A lodestone dropped into her belly.

"Good." He pulled a fresh coat from the armoire—someone must've unpacked his luggage—and pulled it on over his impressive biceps, covering his hard, broad chest. She almost mewled in distress. "I am expected at a meeting in thirty minutes," he said off-hand, as if he didn't just gut her and rob her of the happiness she'd been nursing since her orgasm.

That nausea that had cursed her during the first part of their flight to Malaysia returned full force, and she swallowed down the bile that rose into her throat.

This shouldn't bother you. He never promised to be a good husband. No, he'd only went on about desiring her for two years, screwed her until she was mindless, and then switched from sexy orgasm god to cold, business-like billionaire.

Suck it up, Mariana. This is what you signed up for.

The heat of her anger sizzled beneath the bitterness of her jealousy and the frustration at herself and her weakness for the tall, gorgeous Russian.

Shrugging, she met his gaze with her patented attorney gaze—one that was as hard as it was flat. She'd be damned if she let him know how much his abandonment bothered her. And besides, they were only in Asia for his business. She had no right to be angry that he was leaving to see to that business.

But she couldn't get her heart to listen.

"That's fine," she said. "I'll see you later." Without a backward glance, Mariana sashayed from the room, ignoring the pricking of humiliation invading her chest.

HE FELT LIKE SHIT. HE WANTED TO TELL GREGOR TO TURN THE car around so he could go back to Mariana and wipe the hurt from her face, but that ugly, harsh voice in his head kept badgering him, reminding him that his first priority was Trans-Global Corporation. That Mariana was nothing more than a way to scratch an itch...an itch that had been plaguing him since he'd spied her in that courtroom, her hair pinned back in a prim bun, her skirt tight, her coat unbuttoned, her face lit up with the fire of confidence, daring, and passion. Seeing her like that had turned him inside out. It was *that* Mariana he wanted.

Now that he had her, he didn't know what the hell to do with her.

She too much woman for you? That hideous voice hissed in his mind, making every point of pride prickle against the onslaught. No. She wasn't too much woman for him, she was all the woman he would ever need. And he would do whatever it took to keep her. Expect sacrifice his business deal.

But...the memory of the pain in her cocoa eyes made the recesses around his heart fill with something that smacked of regret. He despised regret. Regret only ever led to poor decisions, guilt, and one hell of a hangover.

Mariana's lovely expressive face flashed through his mind, striking at him like a ballistic missile, aimed squarely at his intentions. She'd tried to hide it behind a curtain of careless chill—like an experienced attorney going in for the kill, but he'd seen—the merest glimpse—of her disappointment. Her dejection. And the loss of the smoldering heat that had been burning in her gaze since they'd brought each other to mind-melting orgasm in the jet.

I made a mistake, the thought blasted through his mind, and the ache in his chest grew ten-fold. But it was too late. Gregor pulled the car up to the hotel where Lyuba and the other members of the legal team were holed up, licking their wounds and waiting for the hammer to fall. A hammer he was bringing with him.

He was on the elevator before he knew what he was doing, his hands fisted at his sides, his chest tight. Tension sent ripples of apprehension through his body, but that only bolstered his determination to kick Lyuba to the curb, hand the Malaysia deal to Milos, and get back to his wife—whom he'd left quite angry and disappointed in their $5,000 per night suite.

Closing his eyes, he imagined Mariana. Before he'd left, she'd been dressed in a light, flowing sundress bedecked with embroidered roses and bees. It was a frilly dress; not one he'd expect to see draped over the luscious curves of a kick ass lawyer, but...somehow it only emphasized Mariana's delicate beauty.

"Damn," he cursed, his cock, once again, threatening to rip the seams of his tailored slacks. He needed to get his libido under control or else he'd have a boner in front of Lyuba, give her the wrong idea, and then spend the next year trying to rid himself of her. More than anything, he wanted the break with his best attorney and second best lover to be as clean and neat as possible. If she allowed it to be so. A niggling sensation at the back of his neck told him that he was walking into an ugly situation.

Pulling his shoulders back, he waited for the elevator doors to open on the 27th floor, then strode from the lift and down the hall to the suite Lyuba had reserved for her own use during the business trip.

Upon reaching room 2743, he used the keycard provided by Gregor, turned the knob and entered, not bothering to knock and announce himself. Lyuba was dressed in her usual suit and severe expression, and was seated on the couch, her laptop and a stack of files spread out around her.

He could tell by the stiffening in her shoulders that she knew he was there, but she didn't look up. Didn't bother acknowledging his presence. It grated. She was the reason he'd shortened his honeymoon. She was the reason he was in her suite instead of his own, with a wife who was quickly losing patience with him.

Dammit.

"Lyuba, we need to talk about this mess. What the hell were you thinking refusing the board members—of the company we're trying to acquire—a chance to review the contract?"

She finally looked up at him, her iron hard expression in place. He hated that look; he could never tell what she was thinking. And that was dangerous.

She cocked an eyebrow and sighed, pushing her laptop off her lap and onto the couch beside her—acting as if *he* was the imposition. As if his being there was disrupting *her* day.

Fuck that.

"What the hell is going on with you, Lyuba?" he asked, planting his fists on his hips, the urge to reach out and shake her nigh impossible to ignore.

"What bothers you more, the fact that I pushed the board members a little too hard, or the fact that I cut your personal business in Moscow short?" The sharpness in her voice told him she knew more than she should about his personal business. Damn Milos! The man couldn't keep a secret if his life depended on it. Just another fucking thing he'd have to deal with when all he wanted to do was strip Mariana bare and kiss every inch of her body.

Crossing his arms over his chest, Vitali refused to rise to Lyuba's bait. She wanted him to lose his cool, to get riled—she liked it when he was riled, because they often had the best sex when they were both wound up. But not this time. This time he was wound up, but not for Lyuba—*because* of Lyuba.

"You knew this deal was necessary to open doors in the Asian agricultural innovations market. If you can't handle the pressure, step aside. I will not have you ruin my business just to get back at me for some perceived slight. My business is not a toy," he said, his voice clipped.

Lyuba's brightly painted red lips flattened into a line, turning her once beautiful face into a grimacing mask of simmering anger.

But then that iron expression slammed down over her face once again, and she stood, coming around the coffee table to stand before him. Before he could stop her, she reached up and slid the palms of her hands over his chest. A groan rose from her throat.

"Vitali...it hurts me that you would think so little of me," she purred, and he grabbed her wrists, pulling her hands from his body. Her touch made his skin crawl. Her eyes narrowed, the blue in them turning to glittering ice. "You used to enjoy my touch..." she murmured. "Who is she?" The acid in her voice made her sound like a snake readying to strike.

"None of your concern," he snapped, his desire to protect Mariana from Lyuba's venom like a vice around his chest. Not that Mariana couldn't hold her own against Lyuba... He just wanted to protect her, to keep her safe. It was a wholly new sensation for him. Warmth spread out from the aching hollows in his chest, and he gasped at the truth that began whispering through his mind: *"You care about Mariana..."*

It was time to put aside the guilt over his breakup with Lyuba. It was time to stop letting the fear and shadows swirling in his mind control what he said and did. He was a fucking billionaire—shaped and sharpened by his choices. And the best choice he'd ever made was to step into Mariana's courtroom two years ago.

Sharpening his focus—and his determination to get back to his wife—he announced, "As of this moment, consider yourself terminated." At her gasp, he dropped her wrists and stepped back, putting space between them, lessening the roiling in his belly from their nearness. "I will provide a severance that will cover your expenses here, your flight home, and six months' pay. After that, you will be completely cut off from Trans-Global and from me." And good riddance.

Without a backward glance, he turned and left the room—and his greatest mistake—behind him. A burning, pulsing brightness seemed to beam from within him, and the smile it formed on his face made his cheeks ache.

Mariana was waiting for him...and so was the future he hadn't known he wanted until his past was finally laid to rest. As relief filled him, lifting him like an invisible flock of birds, he strode down the hall to Milos's suite.

He had one more thing to deal with before he could focus on what was truly important.

13

Blazing neon signs, glittering lights, and the twinkling of lanterns on fishing boats in the bay...Malaysia was beautiful with its weaving of the old and the new. The incandescent and the candlelight. The blaring and the bygone. Sighing, Mariana stared out over the city, willing her mind to stop spinning and her chest to stop tightening. A soft breeze played with her hair, which she'd left loose, and danced along the hem of the peasant skirt she'd put on —just something a little flirty and fun. After Vitali left, she'd paced their suite, wondering what she'd done wrong to make him withdraw from her. Her body still ached—deliciously—from the things he'd done to her over the last three days. But what did all that sex matter if there wasn't intimacy outside of the bedroom? Raised by a single mother—the result of an arranged marriage that went south after six years—Mariana had yearned for a relationship that would bring her a sense of peace, of belonging. Through school and her career, that desire remained, no matter how far she buried it, it always resurfaced.

And it still pricked at her. She was married now, she should feel something other than well fucked.

You expect too much from Vitali. You're strangers. Give him time.

That thought was the reason she'd taken an hour to figure out what to wear, do her make up—light but sculpting, and prepare herself to be the lighthearted, flirty wife. She was tired of being the hard-nosed attorney, she wanted to be the carefree woman who could let herself just...*live.*

She'd never felt more alive than when she was with Vitali.

Her cell phone rang and she pushed away from the railing to head into the suite to pick it up. The air inside the suite felt stuffy and heavy compared to the air out on the terrace.

The cell rang again and upon seeing the name on the caller ID, she groaned. "Hello, Mama."

"Where have you been? I tried calling Mia but she kept putting me off. I don't like it, Mari, I don't like not knowing what is going on," her mother rattled on, her voice growing shriller by the second. "Are you in some kind of trouble, *mija*?" The concern in her mother's voice gutted her. It was her fault her mother was so worried.

In Spanish, she replied, "No, Mama. I am not in trouble. I am on vacation—and I don't know why Mia didn't just tell you that." She knew why; Mia was trying to save Mariana from having to share about whatever affair she was supposedly having with some beach dude in St. Lucia. *Aw, Mia, I'm going to kill you.*

There was silence on the other end of the line, then a deep sigh. "*Mija*, I am glad to hear you have taken some time for yourself. You deserve a break. Take a year off! Take a lifetime off—you have enough money to last five lifetimes."

Not quite that much, she thought. But then she remembered she was married to a *billionaire*.

At that startling reminder, Mariana's stomach roiled. What would her mother do once she realized what was really going on? When she finally got Vitali to Chicago for their American wedding, what would her dear mama think of the man her only daughter had met and married in less time than it took to get a package from Amazon?

"I don't plan to be gone quite that long, Mama. And once I do get home, I have something I want to tell you..." Silence met that tease of information. *Shit!* That contract through the agency forbade her from sharing anything about the details, including where she currently was and why she was there. But, at least she could tell her mother about getting married to Vitali. She'd have to tell her eventually—she *was* her mother, she couldn't keep her marriage a secret from her forever.

Just until I get back.

"Something bad?" her mother asked, her tone guarded.

Letting out a strangled laugh, Mariana blurted, "No, Mama. Nothing bad. I promise."

More silence.

Her gaze flicked to the large windows overlooking the terrace and the cityscape beyond. She needed to get out of that room, to immerse herself in Malaysia and not just the British owned luxury hotel chain where she was staying.

"I've got to go, Mama. I love you and I'll see you soon," she said in a voice she hoped sounded light.

"I love you, too, baby."

They ended their call and Mariana tossed the phone on the plush couch. Moaning with the slow building ache behind her eyes, she rubbed at her temples.

"Something the matter?" a familiar deep voice rumbled through the room—and right to her pussy. Goddamn that man's stealth and his sexy as hell voice!

Thankful for the loose-fitting skirt, she squeezed her thighs together, trying to ignore the gathering wetness in her panties. Vitali was in front of her, his hands gripping her upper arms, in a matter of milliseconds.

"Mariana, tell me." Surprised by the deep concern in his voice, Mariana blinked up at him, a slow burn making its way through her core. With his hands on her, his darkening green eyes boring down into her, and the heat of his body flowing into her, she couldn't think of anything but kissing him.

Talk first. Kissing later.

Clearing her throat, she offered him a soft smile. "No, there's nothing wrong. That was my mother. She was worried about me because... You know..." She shrugged.

A knowing look melted the worry from his furrowed brow. "Ah, yes. The contract keeps you from saying anything about where you are." He grinned down at her. "What did you tell her?"

That grin of his succeeded in making her all the more aware of the man standing before her—and all the things he could do with his mouth.

"Um..." *Think dammit!* "I told her that I will be home, and that I would have something to tell her once I got there."

His smile only faltered for a fraction of a moment, but Mariana could see a wariness sharpen his gaze. "Back to Chicago?"

Nodding, she wondered what she'd said that would cause the dramatic shift in mood. Again.

"Yes. I'd hoped to invite her to our second wedding ceremony." His grip on her arms tightened but then he dropped his hands, as if she'd become too hot to handle.

"Ah, that's right," he said, then ran his fingers through his jet-black hair, mussing it until he looked like he'd just slid from bed.

Dammit, stop thinking about him and bed. Focus on what needs to get done.

"Did you get everything ironed out with that deal?" *Yes, ask business questions. Keep your head above water.* Business was something she could handle. She was the *tiburon hembra* of corporate business. The kick ass lady shark of the courtroom. But when it came to handling men like Vitali, she was a minnow in a pond of piranha.

Turning, Vitali walked to the bar where a buffet of crystal decanters and tall bottles of Scotch, vodka, and bourbon were lined up. He grabbed the bottle of Scotch and poured himself two fingers.

Mariana waited for him to respond, and watched as he turned back to her, raised the glass to his lips and sipped it —all the while staring at her with those penetrating eyes of his. She felt underdressed, nearly naked beneath that stare. It was disconcerting, enough so that she had to fight the urge to cross her arms over her breasts. Not that he hadn't already seem then in all their plump, round glory.

Tipping up her chin, she met his gaze head-on. "Well?"

The side of his sexy mouth cocked up, and her heart stalled —then began racing. Disoriented by her body's response, she nearly missed it when his gaze dropped to her mouth.

"How would you like to spend the next week exploring Asia?"

She held her breath. Did he mean it? Hardly able to believe this wasn't some sort of carrot dangled before the wife, she arched an eyebrow and pinned him with a look of hopeful disbelief.

"Just you and me? No business deals or phone calls in angry Russian?" So what if she was being selfish? The world—his business—had him for years. She'd had him for only three days. Mariana wanted the time to get to know him, truly know the man behind the sharp suits, gorgeous face, and deep accented voice. There was more to him than being a god in the bedroom. Intimacy was more than just a physical act, it was also becoming so close to someone, they can see into your soul.

His smile grew and so did her longing for time alone with him.

"Absolutely. Just you and me and all the sights, sounds, smells, flavors, and fun of Asia," he drawled.

Excitement burst through her and she rushed to Vitali, throwing her arms around his neck and kissing him square on the mouth. He stiffened and just as he was taking control of the kiss, she pulled away.

Now. She wanted him now.

"We can see Asia tomorrow," she purred, running her finger over his cheek to his bottom lip, and then to the top button of his shirt. "But first...I want to see *you*. Naked."

Vitali growled, his pupils narrowing to pinpricks, and his nostrils flaring—like a wolf scenting the air.

"Whatever my wife wants," he murmured low, right before claiming her mouth.

14

Vitali made short work of removing his coat, his shirt, and unbuckling his belt. He'd nearly stripped to nothing in his eagerness to be inside Mariana, but her hand on his wrist stopped him from undoing the button on his pants.

"Let me," Mariana said, her husky voice low, seductive. He dropped his hands, both curious and anxious—what would she do? His question was answered when she slipped her hands past his waistband and took hold of his erect and throbbing cock. Mariana stroked him, slowly, from top to bottom, and back again.

He hissed, his body tensing. "Shit, Mariana, that feels good," he breathed.

She moaned low in her throat then removed her hand to attack the button and fly on his pants, opening them and then watching as his cock escaped its confines. A large, heavy, thick, and throbbing cock that needed Mariana's special attention.

"Take it," he demanded, and she pushed his boxer briefs and pants down his hips until they were gathered at his knees. His dick pulsed, tapping his lower belly and leaving precum on his own flesh. Mariana slid to her knees and took his cock in her hands, stroking it again.

"Vitali, this is...beautiful," she murmured right before sticking out her tongue and flicking at the drop of milky fluid at the tip.

He nearly flew into the next dimension, rocking back on his heels in an attempt to get his bearings.

"Fuuuuck—uhg—ah...just like that, baby, just like— Fuck!" She was getting the hang of things quickly, her tongue lapping at him, following the vein from just under the tip all the way down to his balls. He wasn't going to last long...

"You taste amazing," Mariana huffed excitedly. She raked her nails down the slabs of his belly, trailing grooves along the lines of his muscles, like she was worshiping them, memorizing them. "I like this...tasting you like this."

Grunting, he looked down at her and arched an eyebrow at her. "Then put it all in your mouth."

It was her turn to arch an eyebrow, but she grinned wickedly, opened her mouth, and took him in as far as he could go. Hell! This was her first time, and she was going at it like a pro. Unbelievable. Unforgettable. The sight of this gorgeous, incredible, passionate woman sucking him like she couldn't get enough—her dark hair rippling as her head bobbed on his swelling, aching cock.

"Mariana...." He said her name like a prayer, and then he ceased thinking all together as she cupped his balls and gave them a squeeze.

The pull of her mouth, the movement of her tongue, the look of pure desire and sensual light in her eyes made his belly clench. His hands moved to her head and got lost in the dark ribbons of her hair. And then, he realized an incandescent truth that shifted something in his being, something deep and critical.

Pleasure exploded from within him, and he threw back his head and roared into the ceiling, thrusting his hips forward, and emptying himself into his wife's throat. His own throat sore from his bellowing, he swallowed back the delirious utterances in Russian—words he couldn't fathom speaking aloud. Words he never thought to hear his own mind conjuring. Mariana pulled away, wiping her gloriously swollen lips with the back of her hand. Her cheeks flushed, desire burning in her gaze, she was the most beautiful woman he'd ever seen.

And he'd show her just how much she meant to him...even if he couldn't say the words.

With ease, he bent and lifted his wife into his arms.

So focused on his not dropping her, Mariana didn't notice they'd arrived in their bedroom until Vitali dropped her on the bed. She bounced, then giggled—the sensations rioting through her mind were too heady, to surreal—everything was so surreal. She'd just given a man a blow job, and not just any man, her husband, the sexiest fucking man on the planet.

Her laughter died in her throat when she met her husband's gaze. Hunger, ravenous and dangerous glittered in the sharp, green depths.

"My turn, *tol'ko moya*, and I have to warn you...I am starving for all that sweet, salty, delicious cum. I want to bathe my tongue in it," he drawled, rolling his shoulders as if in preparation for an assault. When he cocked a wolfish smile at her, her heart stopped. And when he bent and knelt on the bed, her breath caught. And when he stalked up the bed on all fours, her mind exploded.

Shit, shit, shit!

She was undressed in a second. Her thighs opened instinctively, and her husband's gaze laser-focused on that place no other man had seen. It was pulsing, aching, throbbing with each beat of her heart. Vitali leaned to one side, holding himself up with one toned, muscular arm, and with his other hand, he pushed aside her soaking wet panties and slid his finger between the folds of her sex. She arched off the bed.

She moaned, an animalistic sound wrenched from her throat.

A low chuckle escaped his chest, rumbling through the room and into her pussy. His finger followed; slick with her juices, his finger easily entered her clenching channel. She bore down on it, desperate for that full feeling his cock had given her.

"Vitali, dammit, you can't tease me," she grumbled, thrashing her head, her body catching fire as the finger inside her became two, then three.

"But teasing you is my pleasure..." he drawled, then leaned down, flicking his tongue over her clit. She almost screamed as the pleasure rocked through her. He did it again, then sucked on it, pulling the hard nub in between his lips. All the while, he thrust his fingers into her at a pace matched only by him in his frenzy the night before.

Mindless, she mewled, keening, moaning his name. Panting and dizzy from the flood of electricity and dazzling lights behind her eyes, Mariana looked down at the man between her legs. He was staring up at her, lust blazing in his eyes—and something else.

Building, building—the pleasure slowly rose from her core. "I'm going to—"

"Give it to me!" he roared, thrusting his fingers into her ever faster, harder, reaching deeper. With his mouth back on her, devouring her pussy, she succumbed in a blast of agony and bliss.

And as her orgasm rocked through her, stealing the breath from her lungs, one thought surfaced through the maelstrom in her mind: *I love him.* Shuddering, limp, she could only whimper when Vitali climbed his way up the bed and curled into her back, his naked chest pressed against her naked back.

Warm, replete, and exhausted, Mariana let sleep tug at her, pulling her under into the comfortable, wonderful darkness...but before her mind shut off completely, Vitali's voice rumbled against her ear.

"*Ya lyublyu tebya...*"

15

"That was amazing!" she sang, clapping gleefully as she watched the fire dancers leave the circle where onlookers and tourists had gathered to see the street show.

Vitali circled her waist from behind, pulling her back into him and placing his chin on her head in an utterly intimate and familiar manner. It felt good to be held by him, especially in that easy, playful way he'd been doing all week. In six days, they'd explored the colorful and austere Kek Lok Si Temple, and climbed into the Batu Caves while dodging mischievous monkeys and their little hands. In Bangkok, they visited national palaces, tip toed—awestruck—through the many temples and places of worship, and she'd spent what felt like a fortune in Chatuchak Market on all the silky, dangly, glittery, pretty things. By the time she'd covered her arms in bangles and her shoulders with scarves, she'd finally had the grace to feel guilty about making Vitali pay for all of it. He laughed it off, saying that if she could spend his fortune in one day, he'd gladly make another fortune for her to spend the next day.

She laughed at his words, but something in them rang through her, like a truth that was just out of reach.

She loved all the sight-seeing, food tasting, and travelling, but when they weren't exploring their destinations, they were exploring each other. That was one of her most favorite parts of their trip. Away from their businesses, the busyness, and the pressures of life, Vitali had lightened up, becoming more her friend and her lover than the sizzling yet chilly stranger she'd married. And the more she got to know him, the deeper the ache, the greater the fear. She wasn't an idiot, she knew that the feeling growing in her chest had nothing to do with the spicy food—hell, she'd grown up using a habanero as a pacifier—and everything to do with how utterly taken she was with him. She cared about him, and the condition was only getting worse.

Not knowing if he felt the same—if he could *ever* feel the same—was making her sick with worry. What if, when their honeymoon was over, he went back to his billion-dollar corporation and sent her back to her lonely life in Chicago, only her new last name to keep her company? What if this was all just a fun fling for him, one he'd be more than happy to end once he had his fill of her...and Asia?

That's not fair. No...she wasn't being fair to Vitali. Not once had he given any indication that this was anything less than a man and his wife enjoying one another. He smiled, he laughed, he joked. And in those quiet moments, when the lights were out and they were lying side by side in the dark, he'd shared about his time in the orphanage, about his brother and their upbringing in a cold and heartless system. He shared about buying his first farm stand in Ivanovo, and how he'd been determined to make a life for himself, a life where he never had to worry about starving or freezing or being beaten and robbed. And there was more to the story, more he wasn't telling. That was the part she most wanted to know, because not only had his life of scraping and battling for every bite of food honed him into a perfect specimen of manhood, it also sculpted him into the man who ruled over a billion-dollar empire from his cell phone.

The intimacy she'd wanted was developing between them... but she still couldn't shake the creeping wariness that was stealing some of her joy. But she refused to let that stop her from living in the moment with him.

And now, watching the sunset over the crowds in Koh Tao, she was more deliriously happy than she'd ever known in her life. It was because of the man behind her, snuggling her into him where everyone could see. That was another thing about Vitali that she had learned over the week; he wasn't ashamed of her, of showing affection toward her around curious and sometimes shocked eyes. She could imagine the picture they made; her the petite and curvy Latina, and him, the tall, broad, sexy Russian demi-god.

Vitali groaned into her hair. "You smell divine—is that the fragrance you bought in Chatuchak?" He chuckled. "One of the five."

She snorted, not feeling the least bit guilty about it now, especially since he appreciated her purchases. "Why yes, it is," she drawled, spinning in his arms to face him and throw her arms around his neck. She stood on her tip-toes and brushed a kiss over his smiling mouth.

He'd been doing that a lot lately; smiling. And she'd been smiling like a fool, too.

Just in that moment, within his arms and beneath the weight of her emotions, she remembered something he'd whispered as she was going to sleep one night...maybe sometime last week. She couldn't be sure, and she really didn't know what he'd said, only that what he'd uttered had felt...important.

"*Ya lyublyu tebya...*"

Vitali stiffened immediately, pulling away until her hands barely touched the hardness of his chest. She could feel his heart thundering beneath her fingertips, and the look on his face was one of stark fear.

"What did you say?" he asked, his voice as flat as his lips.

Her heart plummeted into her toes, and a roiling-twisting began in her stomach. She swallowed the sick feeling rising into her throat. What had she done to ruin the mood this time?

"I don't know what I said," she replied honestly. "You said it, several nights ago, as I was falling asleep."

She could see his Adam's apple bobbing in a nervous manner, as though he were choking on her answer.

"Why? What does it mean?" she asked, and the sickness turned to the heat of anger in a split second. Would she ever understand this man and his mercurial moods? He'd swing from left to right, hot to cold, stiff to playful in the blink of an eye, and she was getting dizzy from all the changes.

"What the hell is wrong with you, Vitali?" Mariana snapped, and he recoiled as if she'd slapped him. *I should have!*

"Nothing. I was just shocked to hear you say that." This time, when he spoke, his voice was tight, his expression taut. "Let's just forget about it." Before she could tell him to kiss her ass, he grabbed her hand and pulled her through the dispersing crowds toward a taxi stand. He opened the door to the first taxi, sat down, and dragged her in after him.

"Stop pulling on me!" Mariana shook off Vitali's arm. "And I wish you'd stop switching from fire to ice every five seconds. I can't figure out what I'm supposed to say or how I'm supposed to act from moment to moment, and it's driving me fucking nuts!" Panting, her rage boiling over, she clamped her mouth shut lest she say something she'd truly regret. Instead of completing her rant, she crossed her arms over her chest, and turned to peer out the window at the temples, huts, market stands, and colorfully dressed people whizzing by.

He didn't bother saying another word until they were back in their hotel room, and the weight of what was left unsaid was hanging over them like a thundercloud ready to douse them in acid rain.

Plunging his fingers through his hair, he strode to the bar and helped himself to a glass of Scotch. He threw it back and grimaced as the burn hit his throat. She watched, waiting, her heart pounding against her ribs.

Mariana couldn't help the feeling of dread mounting within her, the sense that something was about to happen that would rip her world to shreds. And she hated not being in control of her emotions, her thoughts, her own fucking life —for the first time since she graduated high school.

Vitali sucked in a deep breath, turned back toward her and pinned her with cold, dull, lifeless green eyes.

"I think it's time we take you home," he announced, and an invisible blade pierced her chest.

"Back to Moscow?" she asked, knowing full well what he would say but hoping she was wrong.

His brows furrowing, he pinched the bridge of his nose and squeezed his eyes shut, perhaps trying to shut out the sight of her—to brace himself for what he had to say next.

"No. Back to Chicago," he murmured, then opened his eyes. Two green shards of ice stared back at her. "This is over."

16

"It hurts so much, brother," the little voice sobbed, the sound lost in the darkness of the damp basement where their "uncle" had thrown them. "It hurts so bad, Vitali."

Pulling the trembling body into his own, to try and offer some warmth—even if his own body was racked with cold—Vitali closed his eyes and screamed every curse word he knew into the echoing silence of his mind.

"I know it hurts, Dmitri. I hurt, too," he muttered, sucking back a gasp at the chilly blast of air pushing in through the cracks in the cinderblock walls. "But we can't just give up, not now that we're so close." Staring down at the threadbare blanket pulled up around their shoulders, Vitali let the anger that had been keeping him warm for two months spill over. "We're going to get out of here, we're going to find someplace where we don't have to fight for our food. A place where I can put a coat around your shoulders. A place where I can put caviar and steak in your belly. A place where we never have to count on anyone but ourselves..."

Dmitri shuddered against him, burying his face in Vitali's chest. "That sounds good, brother..." As Dimitri's shallow breaths evened out, Vitali placed a cold hand on his brother's pale cheek. At only five years old, Dmitri couldn't possibly understand the true terror of what was coming, of what their "uncle" had planned for them. Some of the other orphans called the man Sobachiy Yedok, *or Dog Eater, because he treated all the children in his home like dogs. Making them fight one another for scraps of week-old food, making them fight in matches where people paid to watch, betting on which boy would die first.*

It was his fault he and Dmitri were there. He'd trusted the man with the kind face, the one with the fuzzy gray eyebrows, big toothy smile, and a handful of rubles. And a mouth full of lies. He'd promised to be their "uncle," to take the place of the father they'd lost, and he'd almost convinced the headmistress of the orphanage to let him take the boys. But she'd offered Vitali the choice.

And he'd chosen wrong. Now he and Dmitri were nothing more than rabid pups, waiting for their master to chain them in the ring.

Closing his eyes and pulling his brother all the closer, he murmured into Dimitri's ink black hair, "I swear to God I will never let another person hurt us."

THE ANTIQUE ANALOG CLOCK ON THE MANTLE CHIMED THE tenth hour—on the tenth day since he had dropped Mariana at the airport, and watched her climb those stairs to the jet door.

Vitali stared down at the lushly carpeted floor, his head clasped between his hands as he leaned over his knees, the weight of the world pressing down on his shoulders. No... not the weight of the world...the weight of his mistakes.

Like ever contacting the Diamond Bridal Agency. Like ever making Mariana marry him in the first place. Like ever making love to her. Ever allowing her to slip past his defenses and make him feel things for her. Like allowing his fear of the unknown to sour that moment in Koh Tao, when she looked up at him with such warmth and emotion in her eyes and said: "I love you" in Russian.

Shuddering at the memory of what those three simple words had done to him, he closed his eyes and tried to banish the *other* memory—the one of Mariana's face as she climbed the stairs to the jet and turned her back on him. The look of disappointment...betrayal...of hurt.

He'd hurt her, he'd known he would, and he didn't know how to break things off with her without there being some pain. He'd never been good at relationships, and he was a fool to think that just because he wanted her so much upon first sight, things would be different with her.

That wasn't the case. He still felt strangled by the fear of losing a part of himself, a part he'd protected so viciously in the past. A part of himself he didn't know if he still possessed. Was it in there, behind the mile-high steel walls encasing his heart? Was anything still alive in there?

His thoughts jumped to that night, after the body melting sex, and lying next to Mariana, her body curled into his, his arms around her. It had felt so good. Perfect. He remembered thinking how right it felt to have her there. His wife.

Mariana Sanchez-Pavlovich—she'd insisted on keeping her maiden name for professional purposes. His Mariana, the firecracker, the courtroom queen, the amazing and stunning and sensual and beautiful... And then he'd begun falling asleep, thinking of her, feeling her soft breathing, wanting her... He must've spoken those three little words as he drifted off.

The three little words he'd never thought to say to anyone, not even his own brother. But he'd said them to Mariana.

Sucking in a breath, he held it, allowing it to burn his lungs, fighting to regain even an ounce of his control, the same control he'd used to build his billion-dollar business.

A knock on the door of his hotel suite made him grunt. He didn't want to see anyone, didn't want to hear anyone's voice. He'd even chosen to stay in a hotel in Hong Kong instead of returning to his estate in St. Petersburg because he couldn't stand looking at all the faces of the people Mariana would have met, if he'd had the goddamn guts to keep her.

Cursing at his own thoughts, he shot to his feet and marched to the door, ready to throw whoever it was out of his fucking life. He pulled the door open and found a stranger there. He was dressed in a navy-blue uniform with a button-down shirt, knee-length shorts, and an emblem over his chest that read: Rocket Couriers.

"Mr. Vitali Pavlovich?" the man asked, and Vitali nodded. The man held out a bound envelope and a clipboard. "Please sign here."

Confused and still hungover from last night's pity party, he did as bid, taking the package and closing the door in the man's face.

He walked to the couch where he'd been sitting, sleeping, moping, spinning out, and sat down again.

The envelope was from Moscow. From the registry office in Moscow. He was in Hong Kong, where his Asian headquarters were located. *Who* was sending him *what* from Russia?

A niggling, dreadful feeling skittered up his spine. He tore open the envelope and pulled out a thick packet of papers.

They were divorce papers.

Signed by Mariana Sanchez.

As realization slammed into him, he threw his head back and roared into the ceiling, every nerve in his body firing off, and every inch of his skin going taut. And despite the chaos ravaging his body, his mind cleared in a blink.

No! She was divorcing him—leaving him! Suddenly, everything within him went quiet, and the truth he'd been warring against finally smashed through that steel wall around his heart. The truth his subconscious had already acknowledged: *"Ya lyublyu tebya..."*

Staring down at the paper lodestone in his hands, a plan began to form in his mind.

"Fuck this," he growled, right before ripping the packet to shreds.

MARIANA HIT SEND ON YET ANOTHER REPLY TO YET ANOTHER email—one of the 25,000 she'd received while on her *honeymoon.*

Her heart lurched; just the thought of the word made her sick all over again. It hadn't been a honeymoon, it had been a wedding-ring fling, one she'd needed to get over so she could focus on what was real, what she could control, what she was good at.

But she couldn't stop the memories and emotions from flooding her, from reaching down inside of her and ripping her to pieces over and over again. Once she'd returned to Chicago, she'd run straight to Mia—fuck that contract, Vitali broke it, anyway!—and spilled everything to her. Mia was shocked, then angry, then eager to supply them both with copious amounts of wine and chocolate. For three days, Mariana wallowed in her pain, sucking her proverbial thumb while silently railing at the betrayal of her own heart.

She'd fallen, head over heels, for Vitali.

And he'd fallen over his own feet to get rid of her. It was that thought that had bolstered her resolve to get off Mia's couch and get back to her own life. First, she'd have to take a shower, then she'd have to contact the Diamond Bridal Agency about the change in status, then she'd write off the last two weeks of her life and never look back.

That had been a week ago, and she was still trying to face forward, to put Vitali and their hot, heavy, and utterly heart-breaking affair in the past.

"Shit!" she blurted, pushing away from her desk to pace to the large floor-to-ceiling windows on the other side of her humongous office. An office she once believed to be her fortress, her bulwark against the world, her towering castle over all she'd earned—money, accolades, that spot on the best 30 under 30 list. But now...it was just a big, cold, empty space—her office and her heart. It was 9 AM, just after the morning rush, and the city below her was teeming with people, cars, and all the busyness that usually brought her a sense of accomplishment. Now, all it brought her was the gut-wrenching reality that she was alone amidst it all.

Mariana couldn't pinpoint where it had begun to fall apart. Maybe it was when Vitali had decided on a true honeymoon in Asia. Maybe it was when she'd finally begun to weaken her defenses against him—and when he started strengthening his against her. Maybe it was when she'd recited his own words back at him, words she still didn't know the meaning to.

"Ya lyublyu tebya..."

"I love you, too," Mia's voice from behind her brought her around. And then the words she'd said sank in.

"What did you say?" she asked, her chest burning from holding in a gasp.

Mia smiled. "I love you, too. I was responding to what you said. It's in Russian, right? Anton used to say that to me all the time—well, before I got pregnant with Bonita, and he split." Mia walked to Mariana's desk and tossed a pile of mail into Mariana's inbox.

Stunned by Mia's unintended revelation, Mariana slunk to her desk and slid down into her leather chair. How could she have forgotten that Mia had been in love with Anton, the Russian gymnast she'd met while taking yoga downtown?

"*Ya lyublyu tebya* means 'I love you'?" Disbelief held back the hope that pushed its head up over the surface of her agony.

Mia, sensing Mariana's distress, lost her smile. She rushed to Mariana's side and squatted to meet her eye level. "What's wrong, *mi hermana*?" Mia had called her *sister*, because they *were* sisters—blood or no.

"Why would Vitali say that if he didn't mean it?" Mariana said, a sob escaping behind the words. "Why would he tell me he loved me and then end things when I accidently said it back?"

"What do you mean *accidentally*?" Mia asked, her eyes wide with concern and curiosity.

After taking a deep breath and wiping her eyes with a tissue, Mariana told Mia about that last day in Koh Tao, and how she'd simply repeated what she'd heard Vitali say as she was falling asleep.

Mia snorted. "It sounds like he thought he could play at being a husband, even practiced saying the words, but when it came down to it, he didn't have the balls to actually mean any of it." The anger and acid in Mia's voice tore open a new wound in Mariana's heart, and the tears spilled in earnest again.

Mariana didn't know how long she cried into her friend's shoulder, but when a knock on the door broke the soggy trance, she looked up to find Mia's assistant, Margo, standing there.

"Ms. Sanchez, sorry to interrupt, but—" The woman looked flushed and flustered, which was never a good thing. "There's a man in the waiting room..." Margo swallowed then finished, "He says he's your husband."

17

Hands in his trouser pockets and heart in his throat, Vitali watched the slight woman with the severe bun and pinched features walk down a long hallway toward Mariana's office, her feet shuffling quickly. Once he'd announced himself as Mariana's husband, the woman seemed more than eager enough to relay his message, despite the look of shock and wariness on her face.

Standing there, in the plush yet elegant waiting room of Mariana's law offices, Vitali couldn't stop his thoughts from spinning, and his soul from aching for the woman so close yet so far. He'd fucked things up—tore them to pieces and then pissed all over them, but he hoped to God Mariana would forgive him. That she would find it in her heart to give him a second chance, the chance to make her want to say those three little words again—this time, for real.

Several moments later, the woman appeared from the office and shuffled back toward Vitali, her face red, her eyes narrowed, and her hands in fists. She was like a mother hen, coming to peck at the dangerous intruder who dared to threaten her chick.

Dammit. He'd known that the chances of a warm reception were a trillion to one, but he had to take the risk.

The woman stopped right in front of him and peered up at him, her face tight.

"You get ten minutes—no more. Then, I will come in there and drag you out myself," the little hen murmured menacingly before stepping back and away to allow him to pass. He peered down the hallway and saw a tall, lithe, dark-haired woman appear. She was glaring daggers at him. She nodded at him, indicating for him to come at his own peril.

Peril be damned! His wife was in there and he wanted to—no, *needed to*—see her again.

He strode down the hallway and right by the other angry woman and into a large office. The door shut behind him, leaving him holding his breath, waiting for his heart to begin beating again.

You're here, she's here... Make things right.

He couldn't spot Mariana at first because the sun was glinting off the chrome and glass of the buildings opposite and filling the room with brilliant rays of light. But then, he saw her, standing with her back to him, staring out over Chicago.

From the set of her shoulders and the stiffness in her frame, he knew she was holding back. But he didn't want her to hold back, he wanted her—her fire, her tears, her pain, her happiness, her joy—everything. He'd been a moron to believe that he could let her walk away and not miss her. Not want to come crawling back to her on his belly.

She was everything to him, and it had taken those fucking divorce papers to make him realize what he'd be losing.

As if sensing his inner turmoil, Mariana spun on her 4-inch black heels and faced him. Her eyes were glittering, her cheeks were flushed, and her lips were pursed.

Dressed in a light blue dress that hugged every inch of her luscious curves, Mariana looked about as delectable as any dessert he'd ever tasted. God, he needed to taste her again, to feel her coming apart in his arms.

One step at a time, Vitali, his mind screamed, but his cock didn't listen. Hoping to keep her focus on his face, Vitali walked closer, stopping just beside her large immaculate desk.

Mariana's gaze followed him, wariness and hurt burning in those chocolate depths.

"If you're here for a consultation, I'm afraid I have to decline. I no longer do business with Russian clients." Her husky voice absolutely wrecked him. God, how was is possible to miss someone's voice so much?

Coughing to free his own voice from the vice of his longing, Vitali ran his hand over his face. "Well, I suppose it was too much to think we could talk outside of business," he said, his tone as light as he could make it.

She arched an articulate eyebrow. "Yes, it was. There is only business between us now, Mr. Pavlovich. I hope you received the documentation I sent via my attorneys in Moscow," she drawled, planting her hands on her generous hips.

Fuck me... Even when she was pissed she was gorgeous.

"Yes. The divorce papers..." The words were like rotten meat on his tongue. "I got them." He took a step closer to her. "You signed them," he added, still unwilling to believe that she felt so little for him that she would initiate a divorce and sign the goddamn papers without even trying to reach out to him.

She nodded once then crossed her arms over her chest. If he hadn't been looking so intently, he might have missed the flicker of disappointment in her eyes, right before the chilly demeanor returned.

"I suppose you can have your people file them, since you'll be returning there," she turned her back on him, walking toward the windows, dismissing him.

"Good day, Mr. Pavlovich," she intoned.

Stunned but not really surprised by her dismissal, Vitali remained where he stood. Desperation forced the words from his mouth, but his feelings for her lit them on fire.

"I tore them up."

Mariana gasped and spun on her heel once more.

"What!" she blurted. "Why would you do that?"

At the look of surprise on her face—her wide eyes, her mouth open—he knew he'd struck something vital.

Maybe she loves me. Maybe I haven't fucked this up too much to save...

"I had to do it, Mariana," he replied, taking a step toward her, his arms vibrating with the need to reach out and enfold her within them.

She shook her head, her brow furrowing in confusion. "You had to? That doesn't make any sense, Vitali. Why would you tear up your ticket to freedom from the wife you thought you wanted but didn't *actually* want?" She threw that in his face, the hurt from his actions making the words as sharp as knives.

"*Ya lyublyu tebya.*" They weren't just words to him anymore, they were a declaration. And he'd meant every syllable.

He didn't know what to expect, but he did not expect the color to drain from her face, and the light that usually lit her eyes to quickly extinguish.

"Mariana, *moya lyubov*," he said softly, taking another step forward, holding out his hand to her.

Suddenly, the fire was back, and she tipped her chin up, meeting his gaze with swirling mocha eyes. *Yes!* Growling, she marched toward him until she was close enough to shove her finger into his chest. Twice. Three times. Though the poking hurt, the contact with her, no matter how quick, filled him with a heat he had been without for so long. The same heat that had left his life as the jet door closed behind his wife.

"You fucking bastard!" she hissed. "What did I ever do to you? Is it my fat ass or my thick waist or my brown skin?" She named off attributes while ticking them off on her other hand.

Furrowing his brow, he stared down at her. Every single one of the things she named were things he adored about her. "What are you talking about?" Mariana tried stepping back

—probably preparing to come at him again—and though he relished the idea of a having a fiery confrontation with her, he needed to get some things straightened out, first.

Before she could poke him again, or back away, he grabbed her shoulders, holding her in place. She gasped, and he bent his head and gave her a much too quick kiss.

Lord, but he missed her mouth, her taste. Breaking the kiss, he pulled back and looked down into eyes gone starry.

Yes! She missed this, too!

Shaking herself, she lowered her gaze to his chin, just before a deep pink flush infused her cheeks.

"You got rid of me because, despite saying how much you wanted me when you first saw me, the novelty wore off," she murmured, trying to pull away. He wouldn't let her. He'd never let go of her again. "As soon as things stopped being fun for you, as soon as the marriage became real to you, you balked." Her gaze finally rose to meet his, and the pain he saw there gutted him.

She was right, he had balked, but not because of her—it was because of him, and all the shit he'd allowed to grow within him over the years. The same shit he wanted to burn to ashes.

Sliding his hands from her shoulders and up her neck, he cupped her beautiful face in his trembling hands.

"Mariana, *moya lyubov...*" he whispered, leaning down to brush his lips over her forehead, then her eyes, then her mouth. "I am a coward, a lizard, a dog." At her snort of agreement, he allowed a smile to crack his lips. It disappeared just as fast as it appeared. "For thirty-four years, through the building of my business, and the sacrifices, the pain, the loss of my parents, the loss of my home... I lost myself. I buried the soft parts of my heart behind a wall, where I could protect it from all the hurt I knew was coming. Because I wasn't willing to give up, I wasn't willing to lay down and die. I wasn't willing to let those soft parts keep me from getting the hell out of that orphanage and never know another day of hunger or cold."

Mariana's eyes filled with tears, but he kept going.

"So I lived my life with cold precision, never letting anyone or anything past that wall." He leaned down and pressed his forehead against hers, closing his eyes. "Until I saw this gorgeous, brilliant, sexy, passionate, courageous woman fighting for the rights of a small-town farmer with so much conviction that it left me breathless. I didn't want to believe it, that it was possible to fall in love at first sight, but, Mariana..." He drew back and met her gaze, allowing everything he felt for her to fill his expression, softening it. "It happened to me. I fell in love with you without ever having met you."

She shuddered and then—finally—leaned into him, placing her palms against his chest, right where his heart was pounding against it.

"Vitali..." she sighed, "I don't know what to say... I don't know what to believe."

He groaned. "Please believe me. Please let me spend the rest of our lives showing you, every day, how much I love you, and how much you mean to me. You are *moya lyubov*, my wife, my love, my everything, and I cannot imagine spending another moment without you by my side."

18

Someone behind them cleared their throat. Vitali tensed, and Mariana let out the breath she'd been holding. Leaning to the side, she saw Margo standing in the doorway, her eyes wide.

"Ms. Sanchez...?" Poor Margo, she sounded incredibly embarrassed, which only made the situation all the more awkward.

Clearing her throat, Mariana raised her hand and offered the older woman a slight smile.

"It's okay, Margo. You can take your lunch early, and tell Mia she can take her lunch, too." She had no idea what the hell was going on with Vitali, but...her heart wanted it to be the truth; that he loved her. Because she loved him. She loved him so much it hurt like hell.

After a short hesitation, Margo turned and left, closing the door behind her. The click of the latch echoed through the office, reminding her that she was now alone, with her husband, and he'd just confessed his love for her—love at first sight, no less.

But could she believe him? Did she dare believe that this man, the man who made glorious love to her, showed her a life of new experiences and joys, and made her feel like the most beautiful woman in the world—for two short weeks—actually loved her?

"*Moya lyubov*," he breathed before pulling her in to his chest and wrapping his arms around her. Sighing, she couldn't stop marveling at the steady yet rapid beating of his heart against her cheek. Had he really meant all that he'd just said?

Stop second guessing! This is what you wanted!

Pulling away, Mariana looked up into his face, and the heartrending tenderness in his gaze undid her.

"Vitali..." What the hell was she supposed to say? She'd been bawling her eyes out only a few minutes before, and then she'd heard he was there and the rage took over. But now...she didn't know what to feel. All she knew was that, since turning around to face him, every time their gazes collided, her heart flipped over in her chest, and her belly clenched with want of him. "What do you want me to say?" She held her breath and allowed her gaze to take him in. He was wearing a designer t-shirt in light gray, and it was so tight she could see every bulge and taut line of muscle through it. God how she missed those muscles—beneath her fingers and her tongue. Swallowing, she forced her gaze back to his face, where a lopsided, cocky smile knocked the wind out of her.

"I know you must feel something for me, Mariana," he practically purred. "I can see it in your eyes; how they light up then grow dark with desire.

Somewhat chagrined by his observation, she shrugged. "I never denied that you're the hottest thing on two legs, but physical attraction isn't enough to build a relationship on—especially not a marriage."

Vitali rubbed his chin, his forehead, and finally the back of his neck. He let out a huff, and Mariana realized what was going on: Vitali was uncertain! The confident billionaire was in uncharted territory. The knowledge both pleased her and cut her; she wanted the big, bad billionaire to know what she'd felt almost from the moment they met, but she also hated that the man she cared about was experiencing it.

Marriage was confusing and frustrating as hell. But she didn't want it to end.

"I know I have been an ass, Mariana. And I know that letting you in has the potential to hurt like hell, but... Not letting you in has hurt so much more."

A heavy boulder dropped into her belly at the same time a great weight lifted from her shoulders.

Closing the distance between them, she stood on her tip toes and pressed a soft kiss to his lips. He tensed, probably holding his breath to see what else she'd do. Instead of deepening the kiss as she desperately wanted to, she broke the kiss and stepped back.

"Relying on people who love you doesn't make you weak, it doesn't make you any more vulnerable. It makes you stronger. I know it doesn't make sense—people can let you down, they lie, they cheat, they break your heart, but they also lift you up, hold you there, have your back, and clean up your messes. They can be the foundation you build your life on. Look around you," she said, raising her arms and turning in a semi-circle. His gaze never left her face. "This—all of this is something I built from nothing. And I'd still be nothing if it weren't for my mother and Mia. Those two women were the rock supporting me through all the shit and success over the years. I cannot imagine being where I am without them. If I hadn't put my trust in someone other than myself, I'd still be living in Miami, probably on my fifth crackhead boyfriend, living on government aide, and hoping to survive the next gang war."

Vitali drew up to his full height, towering over her with a lethal darkness in his eyes, one that told her he was contemplating murder. She couldn't help but smile; he was like a wolf, snarling at imaginary rival alphas. It was both humorous and hot as hell.

"I would protect you," he said, his deep voice a near inarticulate growl. He raised his large hands to her face but stopped just shy of actually touching her, his expression, once again, filling with uncertainty.

Eager to feel his hands on her, she reached up and completed the circuit, pressing his hands into her cheeks. The warmth of his flesh poured into her, and the electricity of the contact zinged across every nerve ending.

"I know you would, Vitali, and that means a lot to me," she murmured, her voice losing some of its power as she stared up into the unfathomable emotion in his gaze.

"I may not know how to be good at love, but I know how to protect what is mine. And I am scared to death of losing you." He swallowed, tension rolling from his broad shoulders. "I haven't been this scared in years."

Closing her eyes to block out the frightened look on his face, she took a deep breath, knowing there was more to say, and hoping he would listen. She needed him to listen.

"I understand the fear, Vitali, I do." She opened her eyes to stare at his Adam's apple, which was bobbing with his nervousness. "I know you endured a lot of shit when you were a kid. But so did I. And I refuse to let that keep me from knowing what a full and happy life feels like." Gathering all her daring around her, she flicked her eyes up to his.

He was peering down into her soul. "I want a full and happy life with you, Mariana. Do I even have a chance?"

"Vitali, I am not asking you to forget where you come from or what you've been through; they've helped you become the man you are. But you cannot use your past as an excuse to deny yourself a future..." She hesitated the barest moment. "...with me."

His eyes widened in surprise, but then they brightened with more joy than Mariana thought possible. His grip on her face tightened, and he bent down to bring their faces within inches of one another—as if he were looking for any hint that she didn't mean what she'd just said.

"Mariana?" he breathed. "Does that mean that... Can you love me, too? Even with my past and my mistakes and my fears?"

She grinned. "Vitali, I love you."

Before she could gauge his reaction, Vitali claimed her mouth in a searing kiss too long in coming. His hard lips ravaged the softness of hers, shattering her apart. This—this is what she'd been missing, what she'd been starving for since that day in Koh Tao. This man and his mind-blowing kisses. Desperate for more of him, she slid her aching breasts against his chest, groaning at the scape of her nipples along his rock-hard body.

A low rumbling began in his chest, and he deepened the kiss, his tongue sweeping into her hot mouth to set her world on fire. He mastered her, liberated her, made her come alive with pleasure, and die from the agony of his not being buried deep inside her.

He must've read her mind because he tore his mouth from hers and, chest heaving with each breath, strode to the door to lock it.

Mariana watched the movements in the muscles of his ass as he walked, and the wetness in her panties grew until she could feel the dampness against her inner thighs. When he turned back to her, his gorgeous face was hard, wicked, and his brilliant green eyes flashed with emerald fire, burning her, cauterizing the wound his previous actions had caused. His perfect lips curled up on one side, and her pussy thrummed with want. Her gaze dropped to the immense erect cock pushing against the seam in his trousers.

She licked her lips.

He growled. "I'm glad you sent your employees to lunch because I am going to fuck you on your desk—Mrs. Pavlovich."

Shuddering, Mariana felt the world right itself.

A bright and joyful laugh burst from her chest. “Then come get me, husband.”

Love this story? Get your copy of Eve’s next book in the series: Billionaire Bachelor: Omar!

ABOUT THE AUTHOR

Eve Black is a lover of all things sexy, naughty, dirty, filthy, and chocolate.

She loves to write all the sexy scenes she wishes were in the books she reads. So she writes sexy books!

When Eve isn't writing, she is reading, and when she isn't reading, she's drinking tea and coloring in her adult coloring books.

Connect with Eve: Website | Facebook | Twitter | Goodreads

www.ingramcontent.com/pod-product-compliance
Lightning Source LLC
LaVergne TN
LVHW041040150826
845672LV00001B/406

* 9 7 9 8 4 7 2 2 2 2 8 7 7 *